ZOO BOYZ
STREET CHAOS

ZOO BOYZ
STREET CHAOS

TATIANA

Synopsis

A group of bikers known in their city not only as one of the best crews but also as causing havoc wherever they go. From illegal street races to owning their businesses, the Zoo Boyz has the world at their fingertips. The decision made by Zu on behalf of the Zoo Boyz puts both his crew and his friendship with Chevy in jeopardy.

As the group of five handles different situations, they encounter women they believe will ride for them. When they put trust, lust, and death on the line, it shakes things up within the crew, which makes them question each other. Not only is their friendship put to the test, but so is their loyalty. Some will win and some will lose, but in the end, will there still be a crew called Zoo?

"Every woman wants the perfect man, even if she falls in love with him in a book."

— Tatiana

Trigga Warnings

These Neguhs Nasty.
These Neguhs Cuss.
These Neguhs Kill.
These Neguhs Fuck.
These Neguhs are Street.
These Neguhs have zero fucks to give.
These Neguhs have Trauma.
Brief Talks of S.A
Lastly, they use the word NIGGA heavy!! If you are not down for any of it, then this ride may not be for you. Your mental health comes first!

Tati Thoughts

Whew! How did I get here? You guys really do not know how honored I am to present a story with five neguhs with five unique personalities. This is the prequel to the shit show ahead. I wasn't even going to do a story on the other guys. They were going to just be in the background, but somehow, they talked me into it, so here we go.

If this is your first time reading a story by me, let me say welcome to Fairyland, where real life meets fiction. My stories can be unhinged, chaotic, but they are all fun. If you're already part of my fairy crew, then you know how I do and welcome back for another ride.

The Zoo Boyz prequel will give insight on how each guy is. It'll allow you to get a taste of each of their traits. Although they have their own thing going on, at the end of it all, the Zoo Boyz represents brotherhood. No matter what they go through with each other, with women or the ops, there is still a bond, a love they have for each other, especially the love they have for Chevy. As I've said before, Chevy's story is very special. So, before I just throw him out there, let me give you all a taste first.

Will each guy get their own book? Maybe!

Always remember with my stories expect the unexpected!! Now let's get to the fun shit!! I can't wait to see who you are riding for!!!

Happy Reading Fairies!

Playlist

Y'all know we vibe and read over here. Please know you can add the playlist via apple music by following: Freshiebabii

The Color Orange

Optimism, happiness, enthusiasm, and **Connections**. As well as displaying creativity, positivity, **Transformation**, and enlightenment. The color can make people feel outgoing or **Bold**, and can **Strengthen The Emotional Body**, encouraging joy, well-being, and cheerfulness. Orange can also project feelings of **arrogance**, **Pride**, **impatience**, superficiality, and **Lack of Seriousness**.

Prologue

Zu

"Twenty fuckin' bands gone! Ain't no saving you nigga," I spat as I circled Clarence's bitch ass.

We built him some of the best guns money could buy on consignment and the nigga didn't come through with our bread. I was seething because he played with our money. Which meant words were nonexistent.

"I say we put a bullet right between his fucking eyes," Foe stepped into the light.

We had Clarence's washed-up ass in the middle of our warehouse, hanging from the ceiling. His bruised and beat-up body hung there like a rack of meat. Diamond appeared from behind Foe, singing, *"In my mind, I just want to be free!"* pressing the Glock to the nigga's stomach.

Clarence's body bucked around wildly with fear. "Nigga just shoot his ass! You playing around singing Christmas carols and shit," Foe impatience kicked in.

Preach came forward. "Wait. The nigga needs to pray first. It's only right he repents before you send his ass up to the heavens."

"Who said he deserved to go to heaven?" I said to him.

"You are not his judge God is," Preach replied.

"Kill that nigga!" Foe barked.

Rat tat tat tat! Rat tat tat tat!

He shucked and bounced as the bullets flew through him. Smoke lingered from the holes left in Clarence as blood slowly began dripping on the floor. We all glanced back at Chevy, who lowered his arm and tossed the choppa on the table.

"Damn, nigga you turned his ass into Swiss fucking cheese," Foe cackled.

Chevy didn't crack a smile. "What he looks like now won't matter when he's put on a shirt. We got a fucking race tonight which means we cannot lose because I need all the money his bitch ass didn't pay us back. Now let's ride."

We followed behind him, grabbing our helmets to exit the warehouse.

"Heavenly father I pray he found peace before he took his last breath, Amen," Preach prayed as he walked behind me.

Preach was the youngest of our crew. He'd only been riding for two years, but the nigga gear switch game was something cold. Diamond brought him to us. They met him at church when he'd gone with his grandma on Sundays. Preach wasn't your average thug, he was a Preacher's kid. He was calm, always felt the need to pray for someone, but he had a side of him that could be treacherous. It took a little more than shit talking to pull it out of him, though. He was the calm before the storm. Unlike Diamond, who's been with us for five years.

The nigga played around too much, but his hands were deadly. He grew up with his grandma on the same block as I did. I remember when he used to show off in front of the girls popping wheelies on his bike. The girls fell for the shit every time. He was like the green eye bandit snatching pussy everywhere he went. However, if a nigga said the wrong thing, that pretty boy shit went right out the window.

Foe locked up the warehouse while making a quick call so someone could come clean up the mess we'd left behind. Foe was Chevy's protégé. Chevy pulled him off the streets eight years ago. He was like a lost soul out there, causing havoc just because he could. He always carried a forty-five wherever he went and wouldn't hesitate to use it. He was a loose cannon waiting to explode. However, Foe's riding skills were one I'd never seen before. I called that nigga the lane switcher because how quickly the nigga's temper changed was how quick he'd ride lane to lane on you and before you know it, his ass is ten miles ahead.

Once he was on his bike, we all slid our helmets on and took off. In each of our helmets, we had Bluetooth installed. We could communicate with each other. Sometimes it was good to have, other times the shit was annoying. Especially when Diamond's singing ass got to playing around.

We dipped and dove out of traffic, making our way to the race. "Yo Zu next time, no money, no business," I heard Chevy come through.

I smacked my lips because I knew deep down, he blamed me for what happened with Clarence. "Nigga he always came through before I don't know what his ass was on."

We'd all stopped at the red light.

"Who gone tell his people?" Preach chimed in, looking over at me.

Nobody said anything.

"I will handle it," Chevy announced as he sped past me when the light turned green.

Chevy had a heart made of steel. He and I have known each other since our senior year of high school. He was my right hand like pot and pans. He didn't care about anything at all, showing a complete disregard for everything. Although I knew his upbringing was difficult, he rarely mentioned it. We attempted to understand him, but his reserved demeanor made it hard, so we didn't bother. Chevy was reserve, strategic, ruthless and about his money.

He and I had been riding for ten years. We'd come up with the idea of starting a crew when he and I did our first race. We made so much money the first night it was only right. We were a rare breed of nigga's ones that not only rode motorcycles but had a business of building and selling guns. We were wild; we had money, plenty bitches and if the wrong nigga came across us, we were like animals. Our group of five was unmatched and every time we rode through the city in our orange and brown jackets, niggas knew to make way for The Zoo Boyz.

Chapter One

HARVEY
Welcome To Da Zoo

I mumbled while puckering my lips in the mirror of Lola's car, "Hold on, let me put on some lipstick."

I glided on a soft nude color to match my brown skin. Since working in Lola's Salon building, I hadn't really been out much. Being a nail tech required weird hours based on my clients. Lola didn't mind my rented space being open a little longer than everyone else. She was a young entrepreneur. A mix breed with Spanish and Black. She was a bad bitch too. She owned a few luxury salons throughout the city. Her father had money also, so he spoiled her. Her five eight frame was nowhere near slim. I think she had her body done, but if you ask her, she was all natural. Her complexion, a beautiful caramel tone, perfectly complemented her dark, sleek hair. She had been begging me to go see the Zoo Boyz race. I'd shared with her I was close friends with one member, and she's been asking ever since.

1

It was her lucky day because he'd finally invited me after telling me no countless times. June acted as if his motorcycle crew was like some secret society. In reality, it was a bunch of hoe ass niggas riding the streets late at night, causing havoc. Tonight, though, would be the first time I got to meet all of them. I got out of the car, pulling down the tight-fitting dress I wore. "What you say your friend name was again?" Lola asked, as we cross the busy street into a crowd of people who were here to see the race as well.

"Chevy," I told her.

June never went by his actual name instead; he went by Chevy. One wouldn't dare to disrespect his request. He felt the name given to him at birth wasn't one out of love yet, a name that some random person gave him. He and I grew up together in foster care. We both were in and out of different homes until the last family he went with adopted him. Chevy has been through a lot, and he wore that shit on his sleeves. He knew how to separate the two lives. Although he and I were very close, he never talked much about his crew nor brought them around me. I'm sure it was the same way when he was with them.

We had finally squeezed our way through the crowd to the front. As my eyes scanned the surroundings, the diverse crowd of people gathered there captivated me. The Black Knights were across from us. The black and silver jackets worn by their members were eye-catching. They parleyed against their bikes, talking amongst one another. The people that supported them stood around with wearing the same colors as the crew. We all waited for the Zoo Boyz to arrive. The sound of a bunch of people chanting caught my attention. "Welcome to da Zoo!"

Lola and I turned around to find out where the chanting was coming from. The few people standing behind us had now moved to the other side with the Knights's people. The brown and orange flags, shirts, and rags stood out. "*We don't fuck with you we only fuck with the Zoo!*"

A smile beamed on my face as the enormous crowd represented the Zoo Boyz. The sounds of their bikes approaching us fueled me. Lola squeezed my arm, jumping up and down in excitement. "Bitch, get off me!" I spat.

Hell, I was trying to see too. The first bike zoomed by as he popped a wheely. Then another one, this one, did donuts, creating tire marks on the pavement, filling our lungs with smoke. The crowd was losing their shit. Then another and another one. My adrenaline was going on now. They all lined up next to each other, but it was only four bikes. I didn't see Chevy's bike. I glanced back to see if he was coming, but nothing. *Where the fuck is he?* If I would have blinked, I would have missed it. His bike zoomed by as he popped two wheelies into a donut. He picked up speed coming our way.

My eyes grew because it looked like he was heading straight for Lola and me. There were so many people behind us we couldn't move. We squeezed each other hands tightly as Chevy came so close swerving his bike letting his tires screech building up smoke.

"We don't fuck with you we only fuck with the Zoo!"

Everyone behind us screamed as each one of them removed their helmets from their heads. My pussy instantly became wet. These niggas were fine as hell. I couldn't believe Chev had been hiding them from me.

"Girl!" Lola squealed.

Chevy came over to me, removing his helmet from his head. "Behave yo self-tonight. Don't get these nigga's fucked up," he said to me.

I hated when he acted like my daddy. Chevy was the brother I never had, and he reminded me all time. "I'm grown," I shot back.

"Yeah, a'ight you heard what I said."

Lola was squeezing my hand so tight I thought my hand would break. "Oh Chev, this is my girl Lola, Lola this is Chevy," I introduced them.

"Sup."

Lola was cheesing from ear to ear. Chevy shook his head as he went back toward his crew. Lola turned to me, smiling hard

4

as hell. "You did not tell me how fucking fine he was. Goddamn!"

Chevy was fine, but I didn't see him in that light. He had always been the little boy who had nothing to me. I directed my attention from Lola back to the Zoo Boyz. They talked amongst each other until one of their eyes landed on mine. His mouth was moving, but his eyes were on me. My body shuttered as he ran his hand through his dreads. He held up his finger to his crew, moved around them, and began approaching me. My heartbeat picked up. His tall, thick frame was now standing before me. Chocolate skin of perfection. His build was thick and muscular, with long dreads, a beard that looked like it could absorb pussy juice well, and a fucking smile that will make you cum.

"What's yo name?" his deep voice asked.

"Me?" I asked, pointing to myself.

"I'm lookin' at you right?"

A smile crept on my face. "I'm Harvey, and you?"

"Zu come on nigga do that shit later!" another member yelled out.

"I'm big Zu," he winked as he back pedal to their huddle.

Right then, I knew I wanted him and before the night was out, I would have him.

I just hoped Chevy didn't cock block.

5

ZU

Chevy's game face was on now that we had made it to the race. He was on go and expected everyone to be on board. "We got thirty bands on this shit. Let's not fuck it up. Foe middle, Diamond and Preach you take the tail. Zu, you know and—"

"Nigga, why I got to take the tail put Foe rock head ass in the back!" Preach snapped.

"Preach you know Foe always get the middle."

"God don't like ugly, but I'm gone let you niggas have it."

The Black Knights were the only local crew we hadn't raced yet. I knew some of them and they played dirty. I had yet to tell Chevy that tonight's race was going to be a little different. My intentions were to tell him ahead of time, but lately he had been distancing himself from us. I felt like some shit was up, but a nigga didn't want to pry. We all nodded our heads in agreement to his instructions. Before I could jump in to tell him, he walked off, approaching Nash. He was the leader of the Black Knights and a nigga we all hated. Nash,

6

Chevy and I went to school together, and he has always been a zesty mouth nigga.

Diamond turned to me while Chevy went off to talk to Nash. "Did you tell him?"

"Nah," I replied.

The sound of Foe's voice made us look back, alerting us that shit was getting heavy. "Nigga he said we ain't doing it!" Foe stepped up to the side of Nash ready to splat the nigga brains, turning it into a Basquiat painting.

Chevy placed his hand to Foe's chest. I could see their mouth moving but didn't know what was being said. "Man, Chevy about to be on some shit," Preach mumbled.

I knew he was going to be mad about it, but it was something I knew he would get over. We were tight and sometimes we didn't agree on the same things, but at the end of it all, we had each other's back. I knew every decision I made came with a consequence, but Nash shit talking baited me and I took it. As Chevy headed back toward us, you could see his face was tight as a muthafucka.

Diamond threw his hands up while staring at me. "This nigga scared!"

I shot his ass a look. "Nigga stop playing so much."

"So, you making bets and not saying shit," Chevy grumbled.

I stopped talking immediately, turning his way. "It's Choppa I'm not worried about losing to him. I got this my nigga chill."

I could see his jaws clenched, "Nigga if you lose I—"

"I got you."

While everybody sat around talking until the race started, I strolled back over to Harvey. She was the first thing I spotted when I took my helmet off. Her creamy brown skin was one you couldn't miss. She was a thick little something, hips and ass with a nice set of titties too. However, what caught my attention was her legs. Long, thick, and tatted. One of her legs held a full fucking sleeve. Sexy as shit. When I first approached her, it was only to get her name. Now, I was about to spit game. If I saw something I liked, I would have it by any means, and Harvey was no exception.

I stepped up to her while she was talking to her friend. When she saw me standing there, her attention had now zoned in on me. "You back I see," she smiled.

"You coming with me after this shit," I shot back.

She flipped her blonde hair behind her ears. "Says who?"

"Said yo new nigga Zu."

"Why do they call you Zu?"

I smiled, then leaned down to her five-seven stature, placing my lips to her ear, "I'ma show you."

I was so close to Harvey I could smell her sweet pussy dripping. The way it smelled, I'm sure her taste was just as good. If she knew like I did, she probably needed to be doing some kegels or some shit because I was going to wear her little nutty butty ass out.

"Zu!" someone called out.

I tapped her chin before heading back. Nash stepped up, getting everyone's attention. I jogged back and leaned toward Chevy. "I got you."

I snapped my kickstand back, moving my bike to the starting point, which was next to Choppa as we sat side by side. I glanced over at my crew. I could tell Chevy's nerves were fucked up. I nodded my head, giving him the signal to set up the play. We knew how the Knights were, so we needed to make sure everybody was ready just in case some shit popped off. One of the Knight's girls stood between both bikes. She held up her black and silver rag, raising her hand in the air.

"Ready. Set. Go!"

Zu in this bitch! Go!

DIAMOND

Before Zu took off, I'd sped down to midway point. The goal was to lookout for any of the Knights trying to do some funny shit. I waited on my bike just in case. I left my helmet on so we could continue to communicate with each other. I knew Chevy was truly ready to beat Zu's ass because the nigga had been fucking up lately. Although we weren't scared of each other, we knew Chevy gave no fucks and would be ready to smoke anyone for stepping on his toes. If you asked me, the nigga needed more pussy less attitude.

"Diamond, you lookin' out?" Zu's voice came in.

I shook my head, "Yeah slow ass nigga I don't see you yet. Nothing shaking right now."

"Bet! I'm coming up, who at the end?"

"Foe."

"Aye Diamond sing me one of yo grandma hems," Zu laughed.

Preach voice chimed in, "Keep playing with God."

I spotted one of the Knights creeping up on the other side of the street, on his bike. "We got one, Zu ease up and switch lanes. The nigga waiting on you."

"I knew them bitch niggas was gone try some shit," Foe came in.

I went up the block, turning around so I could get to the other side. "I got it don't worry about it."

I saw Zu hit a wheely as he was getting closer. Choppa wasn't too far from him. I moved quick to the other side. I pulled up right next to the nigga waiting for Zu. When he turned his head and saw me, I threw my middle finger up at his ass. As soon as Zu passed us, he took off and so did I. "Oh this nigga want to play!" I yelled out.

The sound of Foe laughing came in. "Let's go!"

Zu dip and dived through the lanes. The one member I was to keep eye on caught up with Zu aiming some shit at his tires. I switched gears, speeding up.

"Zu, nigga brake!" I shouted.

Bloaw!

"Fuck was that?" I heard Preach.

Zu hit his brakes, sending his tires screeching. It was obvious he lost control as his bike leaned to the side, then hit the ground, sending him flying one way and the bike the other way. Choppa sped by. "Fuck!"

I rolled up to Zu, hopped off my bike, helping him up. "Take my shit nigga we can't lose this race!"

Zu hopped up, limped over to my bike, hopped on, and quickly sped away. I approached his bike and removed my helmet. When I got back to everyone, I was gone beat that nigga ass.

"Are you alright?" A feminine voice reached my ears.

I shifted my gaze towards the voice. The girl leaned her head out of the window. "I'm straight," I told her.

Her curious eyes looked me up and down.

The staring she was doing became uncomfortable. "Damn you never seen a nigga before?"

She didn't respond. She simply smirked and started rolling up her window. "Yo!" I called out, causing her to stop.

Only her eyes peeked from the window.

"What's your name?" I asked her.

"Why?"

"Causing I'm asking."

"Monette. You?"

I raised my brow to her. "Diamond."

She rolled her eyes as she continued to roll up the window, driving off. "*PP8-456 got yo ass,*" I mumbled to myself.

The muffled sounds coming from my helmet caught my attention, making me slide it back on.

"Nigga they're headed back yo way while you over the cup caking with bitches!" I heard Foe's grumpy ass.

I tried starting up Zu's damaged bike, but it wasn't giving. *Come on, granddaddy.* I tried it again and this time it started up. By the time I hopped on, Zu and Choppa passed me up. The niggas were running neck to neck.

"Zu yo ass betta ride that muhfucka," I gritted.

The Knight's other rider sped past me, holding up his middle finger, pissing me off. I sped down the street to catch up to his ass. The wind smacked my helmet hard as I picked up speed. I could see the crowd off in the distance as I approached the end of the race. As soon as I got close enough, I hit the brakes, screeching loudly as the bike halted. I quickly hopped off Zu's bike, paying attention to only that one nigga. I took my helmet off, tossing it to Chevy.

I didn't even let the nigga come out of his helmet all the way before I snapped, "Fuck nigga!"

Whap! Whap!

I began drilling on his ass as his boys came over to jump on me, but I didn't give a fuck. I was letting my hands do all the talking. I felt someone pull me off and one of his boys tried to hit me.

Click! Click!

"This Foe five gone clean you right out my boy," Foe gritted, aiming that shit at all of them.

The crowd suddenly got silent as Chevy slowly walked up, stepping between us and the Knights, directing all his attention at Nash.

"Now I'm trying to figure out if I need to tame my animals," he turned, looking at us, then back to Nash. "That's what you called them right? Animals? Or do I let them out the muhfuckin' Zoo!" he roared.

"*We don't fuck with you; we only fuck with the Zoo!*" every cheered.

I realized then that Zu had won the race.

Chapter Two

MONETTE
The Distraction

I'd just sent a text to my cousin to let them know I had made it to the address given. I honestly didn't want to be here because I had much more important things to do. However, I owed them this favor, and I just wanted it to be over so I could move on with my life. I stepped inside the building, almost choking over how much smoke held the air. I waved my hands in front of me, trying to clear my small space.

I glanced around at each person who was guzzling down shots or dancing like they were practically fucking on the floor. I almost felt over dressed as some females around wore tiny ass dresses or a pair of shorts that was so far in their ass a yeast infection was behind it. I glanced back down at my phone because I was immediately ready to go. I went to text my cousin until someone's voice caught my attention.

"Monette, is it?"

When I glanced up, I rolled my eyes. *Here we go.* I didn't even smile. Leaning back, I pointed and put on a fake surprised expression. "Diamond!"

He rubbed his hands together, smiling. "So, you remember?"

"Uh I just saw you less than an hour ago."

Diamond was handsome. Seductive green tight eyes, peanut butter skin, tattoos for days and long hair that was braided in two cornrows. The word *hoe* was written all over him. Although he was giving pretty boy, he really wasn't my type. He reached out to grab my hand, and I pulled away.

"Chill, I just trying to see if you wanted a drink or something."

I sucked my teeth. "You don't have to grab my hand for that."

He nodded his head. The way Diamond began laughing, it almost made me crack a smile, but I held it in. It was almost contagious. I allowed him to lead the way while my eyes bounced on each one of the Zoo Boyz as we walked through the building.

One was in the corner talking to a group of guys. It almost looked as if he was preaching. Very handsome. Low haircut, light skin, slim, tall, and tatted. He wore a pair of glasses that really added on to his good boy looks. Another one, sitting on his bike talking to some girl. He was on the shorter side, maybe five nine. His dark skin, shoulder length dreads, dark beard and eyes said he was troubled. He was cute, though. As Diamond and I got closer to the bar. I spotted another one he was much taller, dreads, body like a God, but he gave me the impression he dogs girls out all the time. The girl he was talking to I felt bad for her because if his dick game was as good as his looks, her world was about to be fucked.

I turned back to Diamond, who was talking to the bartender. He glanced back over at me. "What do you like to drink?"

I leaned forward so he could hear me. "Doesn't matter as long as it's light."

"They say that light will make you fight. You be fighting?"

Yes, fighting for my fucking life. I thought to myself. Seconds later, he was handing me a drink. He winked at me, and we took the drink back. As the liquor coursed down my throat, my eyes scanned the room again. "I thought it was more of you guys," I said to Diamond.

"Were a five-man crew," he paused. "What you know about it?"

If they were a group of five, where was the fifth person? I felt my phone vibrating but was trying to ignore it. Diamond had now stood in front of me. "Come on let's dance."

With a firm grip on my hand, he forcefully dragged me towards the center of the floor. I dragged my feet until we finally arrived at the center. Diamond wrapped his arms tightly around my waist, eliminating any distance between us. He swayed us back and forth. I was surprised to hear him singing because he was good at it. *Well, damn.*

He placed lips to my ear, "You got to loosen up mama. I knew when I saw you earlier, I would see you again."

He pulled back, letting go of my waist now, just staring at me. The longer I stared into his eyes, the more Diamond made me want to smile. He tapped my chin. "I don't want to hog up your time, but I'll see you again. I always get what I want." He winked, walking off, leaving me standing there.

I pulled out my phone to check my messages.

Cuzzo: I want pictures of everything!

Shit! Diamond had distracted me from the entire reason I came to the party to begin with. Now, I almost wished he continued to distract me.

FOE

When I saw Diamond leave the table from talking to Chevy. I wanted to talk to him to see where his head was at. Chevy was my Ace, my big brother. The nigga that saved me from the streets. If it wasn't for him, no telling where I would be. I was young, pulling my strap out on any nigga I could. I was robbing their ass just to make sure I had enough money to eat and lay my head. If the gun was dirty, I would take parts off and use it on a similar gun just so it wouldn't trace back to me. From changing barrels, shaving numbers even switching out the trigger. Niggas called me the gun connoisseur.

All that dirty business I was out there doing had caught up to me, though. Someone niggas I'd rob found me ready to send hot led through me until Chevy stepped up. He'd empty an entire clip on them. He told me he'd been watching me for a while. He knew how good I was with guns. I could assemble and disassemble them with my eyes closed. I help with his gun business building and selling them to big-time drug suppliers. The gun business was it. It was the wave, but Chevy never put all his eggs in one basket. He had other businesses around the city. Chevy was a different breed. Nigga was into that juicing, planting, vegan and meditation shit.

I'd always looked up to him and seeing him like this fucked me up. We all knew something had to be wrong, but the nigga just wouldn't say anything. I'd finally reached the table and sat down. I could tell he was a little high, but relaxed.

"Yo Chevy you cool my G?"

He raised his eyes to me and nodded. "Always."

"You know we appreciate you. I'm just checking in. You know if I need to, I'll fire up a nigga if I had to," I told him honestly.

Chevy leaned back in the chair. "Those days are done. Only time you pulling out that foe five if it's life or death. The goal is getting money, build an empire and live free. We not owing a muhfuckin soul," he said as he pointed at me, "You know why I chose you Foe? You always been a solid nigga. You got a heart under there somewhere. I've always wondered what that felt like?"

This nigga was trying to get deep.

"But you know what," he paused. "God just never had it in my stars. Zoo ova everything."

"You know I'm not deep into religion as Preach, but I'm sure God has his reason for things. Unfortunately, some people's paths are better than others. I'm here if you want to talk about it." I finished.

He leaned forward. "Keep your eyes on Zu. I wasn't feeling the shit earlier he pulled with that race," he tapped the table and stood up.

I watched as he walked over to talk to some girl. I hadn't seen Chevy with a female in a long time. The last little shorty he had didn't last long. The bitches wanted that nigga bad. However, it didn't faze him. His focus had been on some other shit. I just didn't know what, but I was going to find out. I was loyal to the soil and although he didn't want to share what was going on; I needed to know if there was any way I could help.

HARVEY

The after party was jumping. I couldn't believe Chev held out on the shenanigans that go on after their races. Lola and I had a few drinks, danced a little, and chilled with the guys for a while. I kept my eye on Zu all night. Every time I tried to go talk to him, a new girl was in his face. I stood against the wall rocking side to side, enjoying myself when Chev walked up on me.

"I'm about to be out, you should leave too."

My eyes rolled as they landed back on him. "I'm good. Why are you leaving? You guys are celebrating."

"I can keep you company if you want," Lola jumped in, talking to Chev.

"You can't handle my kind of company. Be careful what you ask for," he shot back.

A girlish grin eased on Lola's face. It was nice to see him interact with someone. However, Lola did not know what she was getting into fucking around with Chev. He was not an easy man to love. It would take a lot to break down his walls. The most she would get from him would be some dick and even then, that would be hard because Chev didn't just fuck anybody.

In the corner of my eyes, I saw Zu walking toward the back, and my eyes followed. "Don't do it. I'm warning you now. He's not the nigga for you."

Eyes back on Chev. "Both of you are close to me and if you choose not to listen don't come crying to me."

Eyes on Zu, now Back on Chev. "I'm not a little girl. I got this."

Of all people, Chevy knew I've been through some tough times in my life, especially with men. I felt like over the years it had built me up to handle things better than I have before. I would consider my skin thick, but Chevy thought otherwise. He was my defender and fought many battles on my behalf when it came to men mistreating me. He was almost like my savior, but I wanted to prove to him I didn't always need him.

Chev casually shrugged, but I could tell he was keeping a close watch on me.

Lola's head swung between us. "So are we hanging or—"

"Come on," he said to Lola.

My eyes grew in surprise. Lola walked off, leaving me there. Her head swung back my way. She was cheesing so hard. *I'm going to fuck him.* She mouthed.

As soon as they were out of sight, I headed toward Zu. *Where the hell did he go?* Someone snatched me up so fast as I turned the corner. Panic set in. I squinted my eyes tightly because if I was about to die, I couldn't look. *I just knew the good lord would not do me like this.*

"Scary ass," I heard his deep voice.

I opened my eyes to see Zu in front of me now, letting go of my arms. I playfully swung at him. "You play too much."

"I haven't even put my face in it and you're following me. Is this the type time you on?"

Now, I felt dumb. *Had he been watching me this entire time?*

"I had to pee," I lied.

He raised his brow. He knew I was full of it, but I didn't care. "What's your real name, Zu," I asked, smiling.

"The name I gave you. We're not there yet mama, slow your roll."

Just by how he was talking, I could see he was going to be a problem. I could have easily walked away from him leaving it where it was, but Zu, shit, I just couldn't resist.

"How old are you?" I asked.

I knew he was older, but I didn't know how much older than myself. If he was Chevy's close friend, then he was in his early thirties.

"We must bout to get married or some shit."

"If you can't answer a single question I ask you, then maybe I need to leave."

Zu said nothing. He just stood there looking at me.

"Fine!" I hissed.

I turned to walk away. "Don't make me chase you," his smooth voice floated in my ear.

I continued to walk, but his hands grabbed the back of my dress, pulling me back his way. He spun me around to face him. "You ain't going nowhere. I haven't put my face in it."

"So, you just out here eating every girl's pussy?"

"Nah I just want to eat yours."

A lump formed in my throat. I needed to decide if I was going to let this man touch me or not. My nerves were all over the place because everything in me was telling me to run, but my feet wouldn't move.

ZU

"Oh my *God!*" Harvey screamed while her face pressed against the office wall.

I had her legs spread wide, her dress above her hips, and her back arched. I smeared my face between her legs. It was exactly like I thought her pussy taste sweet as blackberries. Harvey dropped her hips, rocking them back and forth as my tongue glided across her clit.

I felt her legs trembling. She was about to cumin'. I used one hand to open her lips while I wrapped my lips around her clit and sucked.

"Fuck, Zu!" she screamed.

"Mhm," I growled.

I couldn't lie she was sweet, juicy and dripping. I wanted to fuck her, but her actions prior to this moment I knew if I gave her the dick, she would be out of control. Shorty was fine, but I could tell she was a little needy. It had never been a problem for me to pull a shorty. The problem has always been me keeping one. Every time I thought a bitch was good for me, I found something I didn't like about her, or she was crazy. I didn't want to be tied down, but I needed a good girl, one that was for Zu and Zu only.

"Za-Za-Zu!" she howled.

My head flew back when the juices she released shot out. "Damn," I grumbled.

I removed my head from between her legs while she panted, trying to get herself together. When she faced me, her deep brown eyes held a gaze saying I had fucked up. Harvey was hooked.

"You good?" I asked.

She ran her tongue over her lips as she nodded her head. "I need to clean myself up," I told her.

I open the door, leaving the room into the bathroom to clean my face. When I exited the bathroom, Foe was right there waiting. "Nigga, while you're in there fucking on a shorty your old bitch in there acting a fool. Triece gone nut the fuck up."

Triece and I had been messing around since high school. We were identical when it came to playing the game. She wanted to have her cake and eat it too, and so did I. I had cut her off completely when I found out she had gotten pregnant by a nigga I didn't fuck with. To me, she was now damaged goods.

I wasn't sure her reasons for showing up here, but I needed them to stall her out until I got Harvey out of here. Triece wasn't the calm type. Even if I was in the wrong, she would always blame the other woman. Also, Harvey was friends with Chevy. I at least wanted to respect her because of that.

I dropped my head, then look back at Foe. "I need you to get her out of here."

"Who Triece? Hell nah, you know that hoe crazy. I'll end up putting a bullet in her."

Foe and his guns were dangerous, but I knew he was only talking. "Come—"

"Zeus! Zeus! I know you're back there you bet not be with a bitch. I swear," I heard Triece screaming.

"*Fuck!*"

I didn't have time to get to Harvey, so I pointed at the door where she was giving Foe the signal to get Harvey instead. He ran his hand over his face, backing up going into the room. I strolled out to the area where everyone was, including Triece. As soon as she saw me, her thick ass stormed my way. She pointed her finger all in my face. "You look guilty!" she yelled.

"Get yo finger out of my face."

"Zeus, I know you. You for the streets just like these bum ass niggas."

Preach threw his hand up, "I'm for Jesus."

"Please," she sucked her teeth, then directed her attention back to me.

"I promise this is the last time I'm going to let you play in my face. My brother's gone shoot this shit up!"

I snatched her ass up, bringing her closer to me. "You better simmer yo ass down with all that. You and I both know I'll smoke they ass like bacon if they tried it." I gritted. "You need to go home. We ain't kicked it like that in a—"

As I was talking, Foe and Harvey came from the back. The way Harvey looked at me made me feel bad. I was ready for her to show her ass like every other female had in the past. However, to my surprise, she did the opposite. She walked past me like I wasn't just slurping on her pussy like an icy. Triece glared at her, then back at me.

I knew giving her some dick would shut her up. Normally, that's how this little game would work. She would come where I was starting shit screaming and yelling and just to shut her up, I would serve her some dick and we would part ways for a while, then do it all over again. This time, however, I wasn't doing it.

Her time in Zu-Topia was over.

FOE

I normally didn't let females ride my bike, but Zu put me in a position I didn't have a choice. When shorty walked out and saw Zu and Triece I could see the look of disappointment on her face. It wasn't my business, but if she knew what was good for her, Zu wasn't it. He was my nigga and all, but he wasn't the one-woman type. He had way more important things to be focused on, like the decisions he was making and his baby brother Dio, who seemed to be getting caught up in the wrong shit.

I walked my bike outside, then handed her a helmet. "What I'm supposed to do with this?" she asked, turning up her face.

I didn't have the type of patience to deal with an attitude. "Put the shit on your head or I can leave you here and you can figure out how you gone get home," I snapped back.

The way she looked at me made it seem like I was speaking a different language. I removed the helmet from her hands and gently placed it on her head. I got on my bike starting it up.

When I turned to face her, she was still standing beside me. "Get yo ass on this bike."

I saw her jump. I couldn't see her eyes through the dark visor, but I could only imagine what her face looked like.

"You can talk," I told her.

I heard her suck her teeth. "So, this what y'all be doing huh? Talking in these helmets."

"I'm about to speed off, so get on," I paused. "Trust me, I won't hurt you."

Hesitantly, she got on behind me. I raved up my bike, hit the kickstand. I turned my head slightly. "Hold on," I told her as I sped off.

She quickly grabbed on to me tightly. "Nigga slow down!" she yelled.

I began laughing. "You scared?"

"I don't see shit funny. I just want to make it home safe. Make a right!" she screamed.

I quickly dived into the next lane, making a right as she instructed. "Eeh!" she squealed.

"Chill, what's your name?" I asked her, trying to calm her down.

"It's," she paused. "Watch out! It's Harvey, you?"

"Foe."

We had come to a red light. I could hear her heavy panting. I didn't understand why she was so scared, because a nigga wasn't even going fast. The light turned green, and she immediately squeezed me tightly. "Right! Then another right," she announced.

After riding for a while, she had now calm down some. "Who invited you tonight?" I asked her.

"Chevy, he's my best friend."

That was interesting, because he had never mentioned her. It was a lot about Chevy we didn't know. The nigga kept certain shit private, so to see he let someone from the other side of his life meet us say he was opening up some, just not at the speed we wanted him to. I continued to ride until I pulled up into a nice little neighborhood. You could tell that most people who lived on the block were probably working class or retired. I pulled up in her driveway, cutting the bike off. She hopped off the bike, removing the helmet from her head, and so did I.

"Thank you," she smiled.

Harvey was pretty like the good girl type. With her stepping into our world seems like it might be too much for her.

"All good. Can I ask you something," I said to her.

She stared at me curiously. "How long have you been knowing Chevy?"

"Since," she paused. "Since we were kids."

I nodded my head. "Bet."

I watched her as she walked off, making sure she got inside safely. Once she did, I started my bike and took off. If she was close to Chevy as she said and Zu was doing what he did, he better had tread lightly. The Chevy we knew didn't stand for anyone fucking over something or someone he cared for.

In the meantime, I needed to figure out what was going on with Chevy.

Chapter Three

DIAMOND
Ultimatum

Today, I pulled up to my grandma's crib. It was a weekly routine to come check on her, making sure she had everything she needed for the week. I made sure she didn't have to worry about bills, food, or even going to her appointments. Grandma G was my heartbeat and a nigga a lay down in the middle of the street for her. Following my mother's death in a car crash when I was ten, she took on the role of raising me. I owed my life to both her and Chevy. He put me in position to do the things I needed for her.

I noticed a car in the driveway that caught my attention. *Da fuck?* It wasn't the car being here that captured me but who car it was. "PP8-456," I mumbled to myself.

I quickly rushed into the house. "Granny!" I called out.

My grandma was sitting on the couch alongside Monette. When Monette saw me, she was surprised.

"Fuck you doing here!" I spat.

Her head flew back. "Excuse me?"

"Get out!"

I didn't play about my grandma. I knew how people like to take advantage of the elderly, but I wasn't the nigga to play with. Monette didn't budge, and it only pissed me off.

"If you don't get yo ass up and shuffle them dusty ass feet it's gone be—"

"Chew-Chew, it's okay and watch yo mouth in my house boy!" my grandma jumped in.

My nose flared. "She's here to check on me. They just want to make sure I'm being cared for."

I didn't understand why they would think she wasn't being cared for. "She's good, now go!"

Monette finally stood from the couch, coming toward me. Her medium brown skin peeked from her dress shirt. She had slicked her hair into a neat low ponytail, which was maybe shoulder length. Monette's pretty ass came a little closer to me. The smell of her perfume filled my nose. She had thick lips, a slim nose and big brown eyes. She looked good the night I saw her all dressed up, but in her work clothes with little to no makeup, she looked even better.

She crossed one arm over her little clipboard. "It's clear someone felt like she was in danger, so that's where I stepped in." She looked me up and down. "We want to make sure our elders are being treated properly. I will continue to check on her until I decide to close this case. Based off your antics last night are you sure you can care for her?"

Oh, this girl was looney. "I've been taking care of her for years. Now your ass walking in here like she's getting tossed around like a fucking bean bag. I don't know who sent you, but you need close this shit. So, scribble on your little clipboard," I said, flicking it. "That she's good."

I couldn't believe this shit.

"What do I get out of the deal if I do that?"

"This dick. Now go."

"Chew!" my grandma screamed.

"My bad granny," I said, looking over Monette's shoulder.

Eyes back on her. She handed me a piece of paper. "Pick me up at eight. You are taking me out," she whispered.

With that, Monette walked out of my grandma's house. I'd never had a woman so direct. At first, I wanted to fuck with her now; I didn't know about her. That alone set off an alarm in my head.

My grandma came toward me. "She's pretty Chew-Chew. You need to find you a good wholesome Godly woman like her and get away from those bikes."

The crew was loyal to me. Although we raced and had other shit, we dabbled in those were still my bros and it had always been my niggas before bitches.

I did everything my grandma asked before leaving her crib. Zu called me up to link and said he wanted to talk about something important. I knew he was up to no good because Chevy wasn't involved. Shit like this is why Chevy acted the way he did. Zu loved money and anything that included money he was diving in headfirst, not using his brain.

When I pulled up to Zu's condo, I saw Triece's wild ass walking out. She was smiling ear to ear. I could have sworn he cut her ass off. She turned up her nose as she passed me.

"Don't save her she don't want to be save," I sang.

"Fuck you!"

"Nah shorty that's all Zu." I laughed.

I walked inside his crib to see him sitting on the couch, rolling up. "Big Zu! Waddup nigga."

He gave me a quick glance, nodding his head, then back to what he was doing. "I thought you was done with her ass?"

"Shit me too, but I needed to calm her ass down. Shorty was wildin' last night."

I nodded. "Waddup though?"

He finished rolling up, lit his blunt, took a few pulls before he started talking, "We got another race coming up. This one is bigger, way more money."

"Cool, Chevy on board?"

He cut his eyes at me, "Me and that nigga started this I don't have to talk to him every time I decide to do something. I love Chevy til the day I die but I'm trying to chase this paper. This race gone set a nigga up nice, all of us."

Zu wasn't making sense. "Why wouldn't Chevy be on board with getting this paper?"

He handed me the blunt. "Chevy's money is long, yes, but he picks and chooses what type of money he wants to get. This time I'm picking. I'm putting up our juice business."

I jumped up from the couch. "Nigga! Nah, you trippin' Chevy will kill you. You know how he is about his business especially the legal ones. Zu, I don't know if you've been smoking more than weed but yo ass buggin'."

Zu shot up from the couch and began pacing the floor. "We got this. We're all good ass riders. Chevy alone will smoke all they asses. Besides, I need this race."

"Why?"

He stopped pacing, then looked at me. "I fucked up."

I dropped my head. "Man shit!"

I didn't want no parts in this. Me snitching to Chevy wasn't my style, but he was like a father to all of us, loyal as fuck. "Listen, you need to tell him, or I will. When is the race and who are we racing?"

"Thirty days and were racing Dragon Heat."

Dragon heat was an Asian crew. Those dudes were crazy on the bikes. They hadn't lost a race yet. I believe they were part of some sort of gang. If Zu fucked this up, I knew Chevy would never forgive him. Hell, the nigga better pray he doesn't kill him first. I was just pissed he dragged me in the middle. I had a feeling that things would not go according to plan, and it seemed like the Zoo Boyz would be in trouble.

HARVEY

I canceled all my appointments I had today because I just wasn't feeling up to it. I couldn't believe I allowed that man to put his mouth on me and he had a girl the entire time. I felt ashamed. Zu mouth game was impeccable. I've had good eaters before, but nothing like him. However, the little game he pulled on me, I didn't know what to feel. In the back of my mind, I could hear Chevy's voice. *Shit Chevy!*

I jumped out of bed and got ready to go see him. Last night, he texted me, wanting to talk about something. Once I arrived home, I had every intention of replying to him, but my mind was preoccupied with how Zu had played games with me.

After getting dressed, I tried to head out the door, but Lola greeted me. I rolled my eyes because I didn't need her asking questions. Lola and I were cool and all, but nowhere near close enough to tell her all my business.

"Hey girl!" she squealed excitedly.

"Hey Lo, what's up?"

She handed me a coffee drink as I stepped fully outside. "Thanks, but you didn't have too."

"Girl please we're friends."

Lola was up to something. Chevy must have fucked her.

"Cool yes, friends no."

"Ah don't be like that. I umm thought we hang out more," I heard her say.

I spun around so fast she didn't see it coming. "Please, stop. You're merely someone I rent a space from and hung out with a few times. What is it that you want?"

It surprised her I was talking this way, but it was the truth.

"Well, I wanted to see if you were going to see Chevy today?"

"No, I have other things to do. You went with him last night why didn't you get his number or something."

"Yeah well, things happened so fast between us I was still on a cloud."

I hopped in my car, ignoring her. I put the car in reverse, leaving her standing there. "I'll call you!" she yelled, holding up her cup.

I took the silent ride all the way to his house. Chevy lived off in the cut, he had a bad ass home in Malibu. It held the perfect view of the ocean that would take your breath away. When I arrived, I pulled into his long driveway to see his bike, his truck and a beat-up Chevy Caprice. I remember when we were younger; he had always talked about getting one. One in which he could work on and customize it the way he wanted it. I smiled at the thought.

I parked, got out, and used the spare key to go inside the house. Although Chevy was four twenty friendly, you couldn't tell. The nigga's house smelled amazing. He had plants that absorb the air to keep it clean. It was interesting to see that path he took living somewhat a holistic life. *A thug- vegan, plant man.* I giggled to myself.

"Chev!" I called out as I stepped into the open living room, plopping down on his couch.

"Yo!" I heard him.

I glanced back as he came around shirtless with a pair of shorts on. Chevy's body was immaculate. He wasn't a small man, tall, muscular, but thick. He sat down next to me.

"I see you got your dream car," I smiled.

He leaned back, glancing over at me. "Yeah, a project I'm about to start working on. How are you though?"

I knew this was his way of asking what happened last night. I didn't know if those niggas gossip like bitches, but I would not tell him, so he can say I told you so. I would take that embarrassing moment to my grave. If Zu told him, I would deny it until the end of time.

"I'm great! What's up though, you said you wanted to talk."

He leaned forward, resting his elbows on his knees. "You remember the one thing we said we would do together when we got older?"

I held a concerned frown on my face. I knew exactly what he was talking about, but we hadn't brought it up in so long; I thought he had forgotten about it. We used to run away from the different foster homes we were in and always meet at the same bus stop. We swore when we were old enough, we would take the ultimate road trip to find our actual parents. We would stop at different places to either eat, explore, whatever.

"Yeah, I remember," I mumbled.

"Well once I fix that caprice up, I'm taking that trip."

My head flew back. "Chevy you're not serious."

"Serious as a muhfucka." He turned to me. "I found my mother."

My eyes grew in surprise. I didn't know what to say. I honestly didn't know if I was a little jealous or happy for him. "That's amazing."

I reached out and hugged him. "How did you find her?"

"I've been searching for years. She's in Toussaint."

"Chevy that's all the way on the other side of the world."

"I know but I'm taking that drive and I want you to come with me. Like we said."

"What about your crew?"

He stood up, "I'm going to tell them, but not until that Caprice is done and I'm ready to leave. I don't want no one to stop me."

There had to be more to the reason he was so quick to travel. He loved his motorcycle crew and to make such a rash decision didn't sit well with me. Chevy was hiding something.

ZU

I'd just pulled up to Chevy's crib. I knew I needed to tell him about the deal I made with Dragon Heat. There was so much money on the table I had to make sure the entire crew was in line. When I pulled up, I saw an extra car I didn't recognize. I also spotted a ninety-one chevy caprice. He had been talking about buying this shit for months and it looks like he'd finally gotten it.

I got out of the car and headed to the door. I knocked a few times, waiting for him to answer, but when the door open it wasn't him. She rolled her eyes as soon as she saw me.

"Damn that's how you do a nigga after I ate yo pussy."

She quickly turned, rushing over to me. "Would you be quiet. Everybody and they momma doesn't have to know what you did."

I knew she didn't want Chevy to know and honestly; I didn't give a rat's ass. "Look, I want to get something straight with you," I started.

"Nope save it. It was fun, I put you at the top of my eaters list, though."

"Fuck you say to me!" I spat. "You out here letting nigga's put they mouth on you?"

"Nope just you!" She began laughing, but I knew shorty feelings were hurt no matter how hard she tried to play it off.

"You'll neva find a nigga that eat pussy as good as me," I winked. "Where my nigga at?"

She threw her hands on her hips. "So that it?"

"You gone let me explain or jump to conclusions?"

She went to say something, but Chevy appeared. "What's good!" I yelled out.

Harvey quickly turned facing Chevy, then turned only her head to me. *Fuck you.* She mouthed.

I smirked, then focused my attention back on Chevy. "I see you got that ride."

He looked at me curiously as he crossed his arms over his chest. "Yeah. I'm happy you're here though let me holla at you," he said as he headed toward the back.

Chevy had a cold ass man cave. Tv's, bar, pool table and even a movie room in that bitch. When we stepped inside, he closed the door behind him. Chevy didn't ease into the conversation. "You know I ain't neva been the type of nigga to beat around the bush. That shit you pulled the other night; I wasn't feeling it. We had a lot of money on the line and only person you thought about was yourself. Not to mention that shit with Clarence."

I knew he blamed me for it.

"Listen I had nothing to do with him not paying. Frankly he got what he deserved."

"Yeah, but had you got the bread when he made the request, we could have spared a grieving family. Now his kids won't have a father because of a reckless decision."

Chevy walked over to the bar and began pouring up.

"You smoked the nigga," I threw this conversation right back at him.

He halted mid pour looking at me. "I had to. A lesson needed to be given."

I couldn't believe this nigga. He somehow twisted the entire situation to justify why he killed Clarence. He came from around the bar handing me a drink.

"Now, what's up with you?"

I took the drink back, setting the glass onto the bar's countertop. There was a lot I needed to tell him. Not just about the race I set up, but also how I fucked up and lost a lot of money-making bets with one of the heavy hittas. The nigga didn't play about his bread and therefore we really needed to win this upcoming race. I tried stepping away from the gambling life, but when you were in that world as heavy as I was, it was hard.

"I set up another race."

"Ok. When?"

"In thirty days with," I paused. "With Dragon Heat."

Chevy eyes flickered. His lack of emotion kept you wondering about his thoughts. His nod was gradual. "Ok, what numbers are we talking?"

"A hundred grand," I lied.

The leader of Dragon Heat was fucking paid and a measly hundred grand was nothing to him. He wanted more. It was the reason for me putting up Chevy and my juice bar.

He gave off a sinister heckle. "Zu, nigga you lying to me. I've heard about Tony. That's chump change to him. So, what are the real numbers? See, this the shit I'm talking about making deals on behalf of the crew," he started. I could see Chevy getting upset.

What was making me angry is the fact that he believes this was his crew. He wanted to be the one to speak for us all. He keeps forgetting this is *our* crew, not his. I flicked my nose. "Chev, you my nigga and all, but let's not forget we started this shit together. You don't get to decide what deals I make."

He nodded his head. "Fuck it. I'll let you have this one, *again*! Zu, my nigga if we lose this race. I'm done. I'm out and you can have the *crew*."

He took his drink back and walked out of his man cave. *Fuck!* Moments later, Harvey appeared, peeking her head into the room. I glanced at her as she stepped inside. Harvey's pretty ass came toward me. "I know it's not my business what y'all was in here talking about, but I think I know Chev a little better than you do. Just know he's passionate about things and sometimes he seems like he wants to rule everything, but he's been through a lot. He knows what he's talking about. He never misses."

I folded my arms over my chest, just admiring her.

"I know him very well and sometimes the nigga isn't always right. He has to let other people lead sometimes."

She shrugged her shoulders as she began walking around me, looking me up and down. "Like I let you lead the other night, and you played in my face?"

My eyes followed her. "I never played in your face. You act like you're my girl."

She giggled. It was cute. "I could be, but a man like you," she said, as her soft hand stroked my arm. "Don't deserve a woman like me."

Harvey stepped back until she reached the door, walking out of the man's cave. A smile crept on my face because I was about to have her little ass stuck.

FOE

I'd just lift the last donation box placing it inside the church. I let Preach talk me into volunteering at his pops church for a few hours. Between fake smiling at these old ass ladies and listening to his pops give us a speech about how we needed to leave the streets alone every time he walked by, I was over it.

I didn't understand my nigga Preach. Despite all the shit he talked, he was living a double life. It was as if he wanted to stay in the church to make his father happy, yet wanted to terrorize the streets with us. Hell, if you ask me, the nigga was battling his own type of demon.

"Finally, done," I blurted out.

Preach came into the church where I was setting down his last box. "Aye man, thanks for coming to help. God's going to bless you."

"Preach, man I meant to ask you. How do you do it? How are you in here every Sunday, but out there doing," I leaned in, "You know, killing niggas and stuff."

Preach eyes searched around. "You know God can still hear you right? But it's something I ask myself everyday though, he's working on me. I've steered away. It's been hard but trying to find my way back."

I burst into laughter because he was full of shit. "You need a female dawg. You have way too much thinking time on your hand."

He looked at me with a serious stare. "I'm serious. Dark times in my life caused me to walk away from the church. I questioned God and when he didn't give me an immediate answer I turned my back. It gets tough, but I've been trying to work on finding my way back. You fools though, makes it hard."

I nodded my head. "You still need a female though." I laughed.

"Listen, I've had plenty of females but none worth keeping. God has someone for me and when she comes my way I will know. Besides I don't want a hoe in the streets and the sheets."

We both bust out laughing. Until a voice caught our attention, causing us to both look back.

"Hi, I was told the drive was over, but they said I could come inside and give you guys these. It's just a bunch of woman's clothing," the girl said to us.

She was fine as hell, but not my type. I like my girls a little rough around the edges. She looked like one of those goody-to shoes type broad. She stood about average height, flawless ass brown skin, with long braids, long lashes and seductive brown eyes. She was thick as hell. Nice little ass, decent size hips, she had a stomach on her, but baby was sitting nice.

I leaned toward Preach. "I guess God heard you."

He turned to me, cutting his eyes. I shrugged my shoulders as I took the box out of her hands. "Thanks."

"What's your name?" Preach asked her.

She smiled, "I'm Simone and you?" she asked, looking directly at Preach.

He held out his hand to shake hers. "I'm Preach, and this is Foe."

She giggled. "Nice nicknames."

She turned to leave, then stopped. "I know you guys are all churchy and stuff, but if you want, I'm having a small get together. It'll be nice to see some fresh faces there," she came back looking at Preach. "Let me see your phone."

I knew he was about to hit her ass with a smart comment. The nigga gave no girl a chance. He wanted to be the one to approach the woman. He was old school.

"If it's meant for me and my nig- I mean me and my boy to be at your party we'll find our way there."

She nodded her head and turned to leave. "God bless you," he said to her.

Once she was out of ear distance, I began laughing so hard. "Another piece of pussy gone."

"Watch yo mouth we are in the house of the lord."

We headed out of the church, hopped on our bikes, and took off. As we rode through the streets, I heard Preach come in. "Something was off about her."

"Nigga at this point I believe you never had a piece of pussy in your life."

"Fuck you I had plenty. I'm just not a nigga that's for the streets like y'all."

We'd come to a red light. A car pulled up on the side of me. I glanced over and saw some niggas just watching us. "Preach, keep your head on the swivel just in case these niggas move funny."

I saw his head nod up and down. *Green light. Go!* We took off. Preach moved in front of me and the car that was to my left had now gotten behind me. "Right!" I told Preach.

We went right, so did the car. "Nigga let's see if they follow us to the Zoo," I heard Preach.

The Zoo was our warehouse where we did all our dirty work. We maneuver through the street with this car tailing us. Preach and I ducked off to a side street with the niggas still behind us. The car swerved to the side of Preach. I could see the guy's arm extend out of the window, aiming a gun at Preach.

Bloaw!

"This nigga tryna kill me!" Preach barked. "I hope they prayed this morning because I'm on go. Lord, please forgive me for what I'm about to do."

I jumped in, "Amen."

Once we were in front of the Zoo, we left our bikes on the side of the building hurrying to get inside. Preach waited by the door that we purposely left unlocked, and I hid behind one of cabinets where some of the built guns were. It didn't take the niggas long at all to walk inside.

Bloaw!

I shot one in his leg. The other guy turned to see that Preach on the side of him. He quickly swung his Glock in Preach face. I ran up behind him, pressing the forty-five into his back.

"There is a lesson with every action. I just hope God can Save you."

Bloaw!

He sent one right between the nigga's eyes. I came from behind him. "Damn nigga you could have warned me. Tryna blow my shit back too. Now I got this nigga thoughts and dreams on my shirt."

Preach didn't hear anything I said as he dragged the other guy to the center of the warehouse. I could see he had checked out. See, I was that type of nigga. I didn't have time for the talking. I was just going to make your shit explode and move on. Preach, he was different. He was going to give you a speech. The guy groaned as he held on to his bleeding leg.

Preach pushed his glasses up on his nose as he circled around him. "A nigga just came from church and here it is the devil, the fucking serpent came to break me down. I'd wondered why that girl walked into the house of the lord looking like a Jezebel was it you who sent her?"

Preach paced picked up as he continued to walk around him.

"Man, shit. Aren't you a man of Christ why are you doing this."

A demonic laugh bellowed through the warehouse. "*Aw shit!*" I yelled.

Preach pointed the gun in his direction. "Who sent you?"

"I'm not saying shit!"

I ran up on him, growling like a fucking animal. "Nigga you betta tell us!"

"Do you pray? Have you ever asked God for forgiveness? I have to pray all the time. You know why? Cause niggas like you forcing my hand." Preach got louder the more he talked. "Here it is I said I'm trying to find my way back to the house of the lord and you try to kill me. Now I got to show you, so repeat after me. Our father, who are in heaven," Preach started. The man held his leg, rocking back and forth, trying to keep his eyes on Preach. "Wh-what?

"I said, *our father nigga!*" Preached barked this time.

He began stuttering, "Our-Our fa-fa-father."

The guy's head followed as Preach prayed while circling him. I counted down, as I could see my boy was losing his patience.

One, two, three.

Bloaw!

He sent a bullet right through the side of his temple, sending his head slamming against the concrete.

Preached glanced at me. "Heavenly father I pray he found peace before he took his last breath, Amen."

This nigga was crazy. I called the cleaning crew as I normally did. I then text Chevy to fill him in on what happened. We had now left the warehouse; I had been meaning to tell Preach about Chevy being off a little, but considering what just happen I figured I should wait.

"Let's go to that little party," Preach said before getting on his bike.

"Nigga we don't know where it is."

"That's why you need to come to church. Her auntie be in there every Sunday talking about her. I know where she lives at and if I'm correct, which I am, those are Nash's people."

I agreed, but we were going to make a stop at my house first so I could change. If he was right about this shorty and she was trying to set us up, a prayer would be the least of her worries.

Chapter Four

MONETTE
Serving D*ck

I checked myself in the mirror while I waited for Diamond to show up. I figured he would have at least called me, but he hadn't. Seeing him being so protective over his grandmother was such a turn on. It showed me a side other than the player side he had exposed to me at the party. I'd come out of my room only to find my cousin sitting in my living room. "How the hell you get in here?"

He sat on my couch like he paid bills in this bitch. "Mo' you know I have my ways. What's the plan?" Nash asked.

Nash hated the Zoo Boyz, but I believed he hated the leader more than anything. His goal was to strip them of everything, put them down. He wanted to know what they did other than ride. Nash and our cousin Clarence had been planning it for a while. When Clarence didn't come back with the information, we knew something had happened. I wasn't close to him like I was to Nash, but when we got word, that Clarence was dead,

Nash really began losing his mind. I felt like he and Clarence wrote a check their asses couldn't cash.

I was upset at myself for even getting tied up in all of this. It is often said that in times of desperation, individuals will do whatever it takes, and that is exactly what I did a few years ago. I left college to start my business, but I didn't have a penny to my name. So, I allowed Nash to help me. Ever since then, I regretted it. I was to pay him back every penny, but I hadn't really made a fucking dime to pay him back. The money I had from my business went to all my bills. I was barely getting by, but I refused to ask his ass for any more money. It wasn't like my parents were around to help me because they both had succumb to the streets.

Nash said I didn't have to pay him back if I did this. So here I was pretending to be a social worker threating to take someone loved one out of their home just to snoop around. I wanted to try something different. If I could really get to know Diamond, making him feel comfortable with me. I'm sure I could get the information I needed. My phone vibrated, alerting me to check it. When I glance down at the screen, it was Diamond calling me. *Shit!* I glanced at Nash, who was peering at me.

"Hello?" I answered.

"I'm about to pull up, yo ass better be ready!" he snapped, then hung up the phone.

I knew the way I approached things were kind of fucked up, but I wanted to get the ball rolling to get Nash out of my face.

I glanced back over at my cousin, who couldn't wait to see who I was talking to. "Who was that?"

"Nigga my phone, my house, and none of your business. I will call you when I get details."

He stood walking my way, "Yeah don't take too long. Time is money," he said as he left.

I finished getting ready and just as I was putting my heels on; I heard a knock at my door. I knew it was Diamond because he was damn near beating on it. I rushed over, swinging it open. His green eyes burned into mine. "Is you ready?"

"What's with the attitude?"

He poked his head inside my house, then side eyed me. "I'm straight, you forcing a nigga to take you out. This is about my grandma not you so come on."

Now I felt bad. Although I gave him that ultimatum, I thought he had an interest in me and would genuinely enjoy taking me out. I locked up my place, following behind him. When we reached the curb, I stopped. Diamond turned toward me. "Come on," he waved his hand.

"Diamond, I have on five-inch heels and this tiny ass dress. I know you don't expect me to get on that."

He'd finally smiled. "If you want me to take you out, you better hike that dress up baby and get on this bike."

I could not believe this shit. I wanted to run back inside and change, but I was afraid he would leave. He held out his hand his for mine. When I accepted, he pulled me closer. "Don't be afraid just enjoy the ride, I got you." he winked. "Put this on."

I took the heavy helmet from his hand, sliding it on. He lifted the visor. "We can chop it up through here," he said to me as he flipped the visor back down.

Diamond put on his helmet as he got onto the bike. He reached out for my hand, helping me behind him. I eased my arms around his waist. He took off flying down the street. My heart raced as the night life passed by so quickly.

"Why are you going so fast?"

He said nothing. I felt dumb, like I was talking to myself. "Hello? Testing, testing," I said in the helmet.

"You look good as shit by the way."

I jumped from his voice but smiled under the helmet. "Thank you."

The night breeze crept between my legs as he seemed to pick up speed. I clenched onto him tightly. "You just wanted to hold a nigga," I heard him say.

"No, I want to live to see another day."

Diamond's laugh filled my ear. He cruised through the streets, then hit a few more corners before slowing down. We were now downtown. The LA city lights and tall building were a vibe. "Where are we?"

He said nothing. Instead, he pulled into a parking garage. Once he fully stopped, he hit the kickstand, got off and help me off. We both removed the helmets from our heads. We took an elevator up to the top floor, getting off. "This my crib. Now, for whatever reason you felt the need to judge me based on a party with my nigga's. So let me show you what the fuck is really good."

He took my hand, leading the way. As soon as I stepped inside his place, my mouth hit the floor. It was beautiful inside. "This is nice."

"Yeah, my bro always told me you should live how you want to be seen. So, I live like a fucking king."

Maybe Nash was on to something. Looking at Diamond compared to his place, it wasn't adding up. He had to be doing something on the side, and me being the person I was, I was going to find out.

DIAMOND

Monette making me take her out to get her off my back about my grandma had a nigga curious. I didn't trust her ass with a ten-foot pole. I knew she thought I was some ghetto ass nigga who had nothing probably sold drugs, but I was about to show her ass. I wasn't worried about bringing her to my crib because, if anything happened; I knew it was her who setup the play. I had enough firepower in this bitch to blow her and whomever else to kingdom come.

I watched as she admired my home. It took a lot of races and moving guns to get this shit, and I wasn't about to let her, or anyone, take that from me. I couldn't lie, though she was looking good as a bitch. After she finished walking around taking in my home, she turned to me. "Did we stop here to grab something?"

"This is our date. I'm going to cook for you," I told her as I stepped into the kitchen.

Monette began laughing, "What?"

"You heard what I said. I'm going to cook for you. I can tell you never had a nigga cater to you before."

She stopped laughing, clearing her throat. I knew how to treat a woman because my grandma raised me, but I believed some women didn't deserve this privilege. The only reason she was getting it was because I wanted to find out what she was up to. Now she was in Diamond land and most women who stepped onto my playing field never left a winner.

I turned on some music to set the mood. Monette slid her heels off as she stepped into the living room, glancing out the panoramic window that captured the city's nightlife. It was the best part of living downtown LA. I pulled out a pre-rolled blunt and lit it. "You want something to drink?"

She didn't even bother to look my way. Instead, she just nodded her head. I poured her some wine because I wasn't a wine type nigga. I figured the most suitable way to get rid of it was by giving it to someone who drinks wine, or so I thought. With a few puffs of my blunt, I snuck up behind her and offered her the glass. I pushed up against her so close she could barely move.

Turning around, she took the glass out of hand. The way Monette looked at me, I knew something was wrong. The look of guilt settled in her eyes.

She sipped the wine as her eyes never wavered. "What's it like?"

My head flew back because I had no clue what she was talking about. "Fuck you talkin' bout?"

64

She dropped her head, then raised only her eyes back to me. "To live like this. To have everything you want at your disposal?"

I chuckled. "Is that what you think?"

"That's what it looks like."

I shook my head. "Not even. If I had everything at my disposal I would be fucking you right now against this window."

I could see the shift in her demeanor. She tried to move, but I didn't let her. "Diamond, you said you were cooking what are we going to eat?" she tried throwing me off.

It was too late for all that. I was high, horny and curious. "I know what I'm going to eat," I mumbled as my eyes burned into hers.

She guzzled down her glass of wine and went underneath my arm. "What you running for?"

"I'm not running."

I leaned against the window, taking another pull of my blunt, watching her nervously move around. "When the last time you've been fucked? You a virgin?"

I stood there watching her eyes bouncing all over the place, but they wouldn't land on me.

"Come here," I called out to her. "Monette, come here."

Eyes on me. I nodded as I watched hesitation lingered over her head. "I wouldn't make you do something you don't want to do, but I know you're thinking about it. Loosen up and let Diamond show you something."

Monette began walking my way. I started singing. *"I want to turn you on, I wanna lay with with you, that's the least I can do."*

A shy smile formed on her face. She came up to me, placing one hand to the side of my face. I grabbed her hand, stopping her from caressing me. "We ain't doing no soft shit tonight."

I took her wrist, twisting her arm behind her back, spinning her against the window. Monette's forehead pressed against the windowpane as I buried my face in the back of her neck. The way she smelled was incredible, like flowers or some shit. I smoothly slid my hands up and down the sides of her ass, causing her tight dress to rise above her waist. I could feel Monette pressing her butt towards me. She was ready.

Light moans escaped her lips as I allowed my hands to caress her soft skin. "Oh yeah you haven't touched in a long time."

"Yes I- I have."

"The fucking lies you tell. What else you be lying about?" *Smack!*

I hit her ass and watched that muhfucka shake. *Goddamn! Little shorty got ass too.* Both her palms were flat on the window.

66

"Stay right here just like this and don't move."

I walked away from her for a second to grab something and came back. I place my lips to her ear. "Welcome to the land of Diamond."

I slid the condom on and entered. *"Woo shit!"* she yelped.

Up, then down, hips side to side.

Monette's pussy was so tight. Shit probably had cobwebs before I touched her. A nigga should have checked first. The more I stroked her, the wetter she became. "I don't why you was acting like you ain't want this dick, knowing damn well you did," I grunted.

Up, then down, hips side to side.

"Ain't no way," she moaned. "Ain't no goddamn way this feels so good!"

Up, then down, hips side to side.

"Uhh," she growled.

Monette's ass began brewing up a roar. It was time to turn things up a notched. I turned her around, pulling her dress off. I picked her up, placing her back against the window. I rested both her legs over my arms and dug her shit out while I had her ass cheeks spread wide. The wider the better. Monette gripped my back, scratching the fuck out of me. Her head tilted back, her mouth open, as she sucked in air. "God!"

"Call on him baby," I moaned. "This pussy is A-one. *Fuck!*" I moaned.

She swayed her hips. "I'm not supposed to be doing this," she panted.

"What you supposed to be doing, huh? Coming around tryna start some shit."

She brought head forward, her eyes, her fucking eyes. Her eyes were lost. They were in a world of their own. She knew fucking with me she had truly fell into a trap. "Diamond I, mm," she moaned.

I honestly didn't want to hear what she had to say because I knew she was on some sneaky shit. Her pussy was good, but after this I was straight on Monette because one thing I didn't do was the game playing. She rocked her hips slowly, making my body shutter. I planted one hand to the window, making her leg rise high, and that's all I needed to nut. "Shit!" I bellowed.

Once we were done, I allowed her to shower. When we were all cleaned up, I grabbed my jacket and her purse. "Come on so I can take you home."

"But I- I thought." She paused.

I hit her with a smile. "It won't be none of that so come on."

All I needed to do now was wait. She was going to come running back and when she did, the truth would unfold.

HARVEY

After leaving Chevy's Zu followed me back to my house. I thought about us chilling there, but somehow, I let this nigga convince me to ride with him to his house. Zu had a nice little spot in a mid-class neighborhood. I found it surprising he didn't live with his momma or grandparents. I guess those were the type of men I was used to dealing with. I've always picked what people would call toxic men. It wasn't something I purposely chose, but what I ended up with. I don't know if it had anything to do with an absent father, but I guess it was my preference. I've always been *I can fix him* type of woman. However, seeing a man that had his own was just another point added in my book.

I figured with Zu him being Chevy's friend, he wouldn't treat me like the rest of the women because of the consequences that come with fucking me over. I knew Zu only invited me over so we could fuck, but tonight I was going to do my best not to give him access to my body. I needed to know all about the girl that was at the party raising cane. I made myself comfortable on his plush couch while he rolled himself a blunt. The silence between us was loud, making me feel uncomfortable. I wanted to know if he lived here alone. I glanced around, looking at the few pictures he had. "Who else lives here?" I asked.

"My baby brother," Zu paused what he was doing, then turned in my direction. "Come over here."

I ran my hand down my thighs. "I'm good. I know all you want to do is get between my legs."

He started back rolling his blunt, "I did that already, next?"

Well, shut me up! I cleared my throat. "That's because I let you."

He shrugged as he licked the wrap so he could seal the blunt. I watched as his tongued glided across so smoothly. It was the same way it glided back and forth over my clit.

"I see you staring so come here," he mumbled.

I got up from where I was sitting next to him. Zu leaned back on the couch while taking pulling off his blunt. "I want to hold you, get on my lap."

"No."

Zu gripped me by sweater, pulling me toward him. He nuzzled his face in my neck. "You smell so good," he whispered.

His solid chest and cologne were comforting. I wrapped one arm around his neck, smothering his face further into my neck. "Who was that girl?" I whispered.

"My ex."

"You still fucking her?"

"Sometimes."

His honesty cut me. I didn't know if it was a good or bad. He could have easily lied, but he didn't. "You want to leave now or what?"

The answer should have been yes, take me the fuck home right now, but I couldn't. I hadn't gotten the chance to fully explore all of Zu. "You have to cut her off. I'm not going to fuck with you and you're dealing with her."

Zu lifted his head. "You making demands like you breaking a nigga off."

I cut my eyes at him. "I'm not playing."

We stared at each other long and hard. Zu was big trouble; I could feel it. Although he was a friend of Chevy's, it meant nothing to him. "If I fuck you. Zu rule is you cannot fuck no one else and it's not up for discussion."

I pushed myself off him because the audacity of him giving me rules when he clearly just told me he still fucks his ex. He was basically saying I want my cake and eat it too, but you can only have a piece of cake and I better not touch it. I rolled my eyes as I shot up from the couch.

I tried stepping over him but felt my body being sent backward as Zu gripped the back of my tights pulling back down. "Man sit yo ass down."

I didn't know what type of game he was playing, but I didn't want any parts. "Look Harvey, I'm an honest nigga you asked a question, and I gave you an answer. It's not the one you wanted so now you're ready to shake. Nah I don't play like that. You and I are just getting started. Give me a reason to leave the other bitches alone."

"It's you telling me what I can and cannot do while you get to do whatever the fuck you want!" I snapped back.

He took another pull of his blunt as he sat there, still leaning back, glaring at me. A smile crept on his face. "You gone sit there and be mad over some dumb shit or you gone let me eat your pussy?"

I swallowed deep. I wanted to be mad about it, but the way he said it turned me on. I didn't want to look desperate, so I sat there with a neutral face, but inside I was dying for him to put his mouth on me again. My pussy was calling out to him, practically meowing. Zu handed me his blunt.

"Here take a few hits and relax. Big Zu got you."

I took the blunt from his hand and began taking long pulls. With a gentle touch, Zu guided me back onto the couch. "Yeah, keep hitting it, let me take care of you," he mumbled as he eased my tights off.

Inhale, hold, exhale. His soft kisses tickled me as his hand gripped my thighs, spreading them wide, placing my legs over his shoulders. He pulled me close to him. I could hear him growling animal like. The shit was sexy as fuck. *Inhale, hold, exhale.* That's when I felt his warm tongue on me, sending my eyes back. "Mm," I moaned.

I placed the blunt back to my lips. *Inhale, hold, exhale.* "Goddamn you can eat pussy good. So fucking good."

Zu was smacking on me like he was eating a piece of chewy candy. The weed was kicking in now and between the feeling of being high and his face between my legs were indescribable. One hand to his head, pushing his face close as I could get it, while my other hand, held the blunt I put back to my lips. *Inhale, hold, exhale.*

He began mumbling, "Pussy so sweet."

"And you got a sweet tooth."

"Candy licker," he hummed on my clit.

My head shot up as my body shutter. Suddenly, I didn't feel his tongue anymore. My eyes searched around. The nigga left me laying here, legs wide, wet as hell. I went to move, but heard him talking. "Don't you move."

Zu came back fully naked. When my eyes landed on what he had hanging, I got scared jumping up. "Who you fucking with that?"

Zu was blessed. Hell over blessed and there was no way I was taking all of that.

"You scared?"

"No," I lied.

"You can't take dick?" he paused. "Or you a virgin?"

My heart was racing as he came toward me. "I'm not a virgin. I—"

Zu placed his fingers to his lips, signaling for me to shut the fuck up. "Then show me what you working with."

He sat on the couch, leaning over, pulling me on top of him. "Inch by inch baby," he said to me.

I stared at him, then down at his thick ass dick, then back at him. *Inch by inch,* he mouthed. I went slowly as I eased down on top of him. "My *God!*" I shouted as my mouth opened.

I couldn't even go all the way down because this nigga was stretching me out.

"Don't worry when I'm done with you, you'll be taking this dick like a pro."

He placed his hand to my waist, moving my hips back and forth. He began doing some type of hip movement, making the experience chefs fucking kiss. My head fell back, allowing Zu to lean forward to suck on it. "Tight ass, ride this dick baby."

Back, forth, up, slam down.

"Fuck!" I moaned loudly.

Back, forth, up, slam down.

"Welcome to Zu-Topia mama," he growled.

Back, forth, up, slam down.

My hips opened wider, making my body relax. Before I knew it, I was riding him like a fucking bull. Zu-Topia was everything. The sounds of me and Zu fucking the couch up were like two wild animals.

Bam! Bam! Bam!

"Zu!"

I heard a woman's voice. This was the shit I worried about. Zu went to get up, but I was enjoying the ride, and the bitch would have to wait. I turned his head back toward me. "No!" I moaned.

He nodded his head. Our eyes locked in on each other. I felt my body taking in all his toxic energy. Snatching his soul while he snatched mine. This time, he kissed me. Our tongues fought each other nastily. The motion of his thrusting hips made my body faster. I planted my feet flat so I could really work his ass.

Back, forth, up, slam down.

"Zeus, I know you're in there!" the woman screamed again.

"Hold on," he whispered.

I snapped this time. "I said fucking no!"

Back, forth, up, slam down.

I was almost there, and I wasn't about to let a bitch ruin it. Zu wrapped his arms tightly around my waist, scooting toward the edge of the couch. Big boy was throwing my ass like a slinky. "Animal!" he growled.

Zu was toxic, and I knew it, but he had no clue how toxic I could be, especially over some good dick. The sound of shattering glass startled us as something came flying through his front window. *"Fuck!"* He shouted, picking me up, tossing me on the other side of him.

Now I had an attitude. I quickly put my pants back on, rushing over to the side of the window. The woman climbed in damn near, breaking her neck. She didn't see me standing in the dark. Only person she saw was Zu standing there naked. She started going off on him.

"Who you in here fucking, huh? Where the bitch at so I can beat her ass!"

Zu dropped his head. "Triece we are not together and the fact you just broke my fucking window I'm really not fucking with you. I'm two second from beating yo ass."

Her head swung from left to right. "You ain't gone do shit. Where the bitch at?"

Zu had the type of dick that would make you act like she did, so a part of me didn't blame her, but she wasn't about to bully me. I came from the shadows. "Here I am."

She immediately swung at me, and we started fighting. We were all over Zu's spot. I was rocking her fucking block. Zu snatched me up, taking me to the back room, "Stay yo ass right here let me get her out of here!"

"Nigga I'm not about to be doing this shit at all. Fuck you and that bitch!" I panted, out of breath.

I paced the floors when he closed the door. When I heard the front door close, I crept out of the room. I needed to leave, and I knew Zu would not take me home. I snatched up my phone to call someone. I couldn't call Chevy because I didn't want to hear *I told you so*. I snatched Zu's phone off the table. Oddly, he didn't lock it. It wasn't my intentions to go through his phone. I just needed to get a number. As my eyes quickly searched, I saw nothing but bitches filled his text box. "Ugh!"

I found the number I needed and called. I was leaving this nigga house tonight by any means necessary.

Chapter Five

FOE
Crash Out

When Preach and I arrived at the little kickback, there weren't cars lined up in the driveway or up and down the block. Preach and I glanced at each other. "Nigga you sure this the right house. Shit looks dry as fuck to me."

He glanced down at his phone, then back at the house. "Yeah, this the right address."

Before we strolled up to the door, I needed to know the plan. "Nigga, what you thinking?" I asked.

Preach smiled mischievously. "You know butter her up. You run a little game and they get to talking."

"Bet, so you fucking her for information."

We got to the door, and it didn't take long before Simone answered. "Oh hey."

"Sup," Preach said dryly.

She opened the door, letting us inside. It was only two other girls in there.

"Type fucking party is this? You ain't got no friends?" I blurted out.

Simone rolled her eyes. But I didn't care. One of her friends waved, and the other was all on her phone. "No one showed up so it's just us. That's my friend Elise," she pointed to the one that waved. "And that's my girl Asia." Pointing to the girl that was on her phone. "This is Preach and Foe."

"Type name is Foe?" Asia laughed.

"The type of name that'll fuck a nigga up," I snapped back, causing her to look up.

Asia was pretty, dark skin, tight eye, slim thang. She was beautiful and rough around the edges. Just how I like them. If me and my shorty ain't pulling down pooh shiestys ready to take over the world, I don't want her. She shot me a *fuck you* smirk then face back down in the phone.

Simone glanced at Preach, then shied away. He grabbed her hand, "God said come as you are. A fupa and big thighs don't scare me. You don't have to hide," he told her.

Simone began blushing so hard with her cheeks turning red. Preach liked them with meat on their bones. He didn't do the body shaming, nor did he let us. I fucked with it. Other than the church shit, Preach remained himself. "We'll be back," he said to me.

I leaned in toward him, "Nigga fuck you going we just got here."

"I'm about to do the lords work now stall me out."

Preach was up to something, but I trusted him. I walked over, sitting next to Asia. I could see her looking out the side of her eyes at me. "You smell good as hell," she said to me.

"What I'm supposed to smell like?"

"I don't know but you smell like a whole fucking snack."

My first instinct was to be an asshole, but I pressed the chill button. "Thanks."

She had now fully turned to me. "You ride?" she said, tapping the patch on my jacket.

"You see it don't you?"

Elise stood up, walking over to me, holding a stank face. "Take me for a ride on your bike."

"No."

She tossed her hand on her waist, sucking her teeth. "Why?"

"Because I said so."

"I don't like you!"

"I don't like you either, shit. I don't even know you. Man, look where Preach at?" I said, hopping up from the couch.

I moved through the house like I paid rent. Opening one door after the next. I swung the last door opened and couldn't believe my fucking eyes. Preach had shorty bent over the bed. "Oo yo church boy ass know how to slang some dick," Simone whined.

Preach turned to look at me, then looked back. When I saw what he was recording, I nodded and went back out of the room. I went to head back to the living room and Asia was right there. "Shit!" I screamed.

A hefty laugh came from her belly. "You all in their business." She smiled.

"Nah I was looking for—"

"Nah you were being nosy. Let them do them and you come with me," she said, walking back toward the living room, then out the front door.

When we were outside, she pulled a blunt from her purse. "You want to tap this?"

I waved my hand at her. "I don't smoke other people's blunts especially from people I don't know."

She nodded her head as she indulged in her trees. "Why they call you Foe? I know that isn't the name you were given at birth."

"Cause I be laying fools down with a forty-five."

Asia started laughing again. Most didn't believe me when I told them, so I didn't mind sharing, but it was the truth. I couldn't lie, though. Every time she smiled; it was nice to see. It made me want to do again and again. "Be honest with me was it ever a party?"

Asia looked away, then back at me. "Nobody showed up." She shrugged.

I knew she was lying, but I get it she was protecting her friend. Now my wheels were turning. I went to say something, but my phone ranged, and it was from an unknown number. "Yo, yo!"

"Umm Foe," A girl whispery voice came in.

"Who is this?"

"It's umm Harvey, I didn't want to call Chevy, can you come pick me up please?"

I didn't know why she was calling me. "Don't you got some friends? How you get my number?"

She smacked her lips. "Please!"

"Where are you?"

"Zu's."

Shit! If she was at Zu's, the only reason she could be calling is if Triece is over there showing her fucking ass. I dropped my head. I don't know why she was fucking with this nigga to begin with. We could only do so much saving before Chevy jumped in. "I'm on my way," I told her, hanging up.

Asia fixed her eyes on me as she put out her blunt. "Girlfriend?"

"Nah, I need to bounce though."

She fumbled in her purse. "Let me see your hand," she said, smiling.

I reached my hand out to her, and she scribbled her number in my palm. I don't know why she just didn't ask for my number, but something about her doing it this way, I thought it was cute. I jumped up to go get Preach, but he was coming out of the house.

"Let's ride we got to get to Zu's."

"Bet!"

Preach and I left the house. I needed to get to Zu's crib.

ZU

I stood outside, trying to get Triece to leave. The way she acted made me regret even fucking with her to begin with. Had I known all those years ago that she would act like this, I would have never fucked with her.

"Fuck you here for? Fighting and shit. We done!" I shouted.

She threw her hand in my face. "We done when I say we done. You need to get rid of her."

I stood there watching her act a fool. "Nah we done. I'm not going to argue about it either."

Triece had run off many females I'd messed with after her. The women didn't want to deal with her, so they left me alone. I don't care how many bitches I talked to; she ruined it. Therefore, I needed a woman that was truly for me. Harvey was the first one that threw hands with her. I let them rock for a little, but I didn't want Triece running her off. I liked Harvey. I could see myself fucking with her the long way. I wasn't the perfect nigga, but I could see myself trying to be. However, I couldn't do that with Triece around. I know I said it before that I wasn't giving her no dick and folded, but now that I had a taste of Harvey, there was no way I was giving her up for Triece's nut ass.

She sucked her teeth. "Fuck you Zeus!"

The sounds of bikes coming up the block caught my attention. I saw Foe and Preach pulling up to my crib. I hadn't called them, so I didn't know why they were here. They hopped off their bikes coming toward us.

"Just like yo bitch ass to call yo friends. You fucking them too!"

Foe's faced curled up, "Only thing I fuck is pussy, Zu you stay dealing with some wild ass hoes," he said, now stepping on the porch.

Triece turned to Preach, and he threw his hand up. "Don't!" he said to her.

"Nigga fuck you too! Confused nigga one minute you're in church next you in the streets."

"Jesus loves you." He smiled at her.

Moments later, Harvey came out of the house with her purse. "Where you going?" I asked, confused.

"I called Foe to pick me up."

She called Foe? Now I was curious how the hell she got his number. I glanced at Foe, and he shrugged. "Shit, she called me I thought something bad happened."

"Hold on!" I shouted. "You calling my niggas to pick you up? We don't do that shorty."

"Well, I don't do this. Fighting bitches?"

"Bitch who you talking to!" Triece shouted.

Harvey pointed at her. "See!"

We all begin going back and forth on my porch, not paying attention to anything but each other.

Bloaw!

The sound of the gun made us all duck but Foe he whipped out, turning around.

"Yo!" Chevy screamed. "Fuck is y'all doing?"

"Nigga you can't be just shooting and shit outside these white folks gone call the laws on us," I gritted.

"Fuck the laws, I said what the fuck is up?"

I glanced at Harvey, and she glanced at me. "How the fuck you know to come here?"

Chevy slowly walked up, "I came to holla at you but apparently y'all decided to have a party without me. Fuck going on?"

"I was just leaving," Harvey said to him.

"You were just staying here." I jumped in.

Chevy shot me a look, then one to her. "She was leaving like she said," Triece jumped in.

Chevy pointed at Triece. "Triece, you need to leave," he calmly told her.

"Nigga you don't run me! Fuck you too," she spat.

He ran his hand over his head as he turned toward her. "I don't disrespect women, so I'm going to say this as nice as I can. Get the fuck on, let's not forget who run this shit, I do. Your brothers they eating because of me. Now if you want to be the reason them niggas shaking cans asking for two cents a day you better kick them fucking feet."

Her head flew back. She couldn't say shit. In the hood, Chevy was the embodiment of being the king. He made it a point to give back, even if it meant bending the rules, to spread wealth as much as possible. We paid the Triece brothers well to be our runners. She back pedal until she reached her car. I knew she had something up her sleeve because he called her out. Chevy didn't know her like I did. Now I would have to keep my eye on her.

"Foe, take Harvey home. Preach and Zu let's chat. Foe as soon as you're done come back. Diamond should be here in a minute."

Just like that, those niggas started moving around. Harvey went to walk past me, but I grabbed her hand, turning her toward me. "Call me," I told her.

"No!"

She walked off, taking the helmet from Foe and hopping on his bike. He took off with her down the street. Preach, Chevy and I went into the house. "Damn they fucked yo shit up!" Preach laughed.

"You let them fight?" Chevy asked.

I began picking up shit off the floor. "Nah they fought on their own. Triece ass is crazy man."

Chevy walked around surveying my spot, "I told you not to fuck with her to begin with. You know she fuckin Nash."

I didn't know. "Fuck you mean?"

"She's fuckin Nash! If yo head wasn't in the pussy, you would have known. Nigga I don't know what's been with you lately between making fucked up decisions that we all have to pay for and that money hungry mindset, shit ain't right."

The pot calling the kettle black. Chevy couldn't be serious right now.

"Says the same nigga who has been distancing himself from the crew. The nigga that was about getting money now scared to make money. The nigga who would never turn down a race but scared to race."

Chevy flicked his nose raising his chin, "Zu my nigga, I'm really feeling like you got some shit you need to get off your chest. Let's not forget how I get down."

Chevy was talking real spicy. He and I had never bumped heads this bad before, but the nigga didn't run me. I was trying to do something for the crew, but he acted as if I was doing this for myself.

"What you come here for? To talk shit? Honestly, if it ain't about why you been acting strange or racing I don't give a fuck!" I barked.

He had now stepped up to me. Chevy and I stood eye to eye. Something was up because the nigga had never been so uptight. "Racing ain't never been the problem, but you sure talking a lot of shit. You want to put yo money where yo mouth is? Cause right about now, I don't have shit to lose. You out here moving reckless. You got these women in here fighting, placing side bets and you talking about some shit I said I was cool with. So, what's good?"

Preach stood between us, "Let's simmer down and figure this shit out. We're brothers. Chev, my nigga you have been acting weird as hell. Zu nigga well, shit, you be moving funny." Preach shrugged. "Let's pray about it. God always know what to do."

I waved Preach off. "Nah, the nigga wants to race. Let's race. How much you got on it?"

"Ten bands and my bike," Chevy said.

I couldn't believe he would put up his bike. That alone spoke volumes. I sat on the couch, "Nah get the fuck up meet me outside!" Chevy demanded.

I shot up from the couch, snatching up my bike keys. "Fuck it!"

We headed outside with Preach behind us. "We really about to do this?" I heard him say.

Chevy wasn't about to back down. As we moved out to the street, Diamond was pulling up. He quickly stopped his bike in front of us, hopping off. "Fuck y'all nigga's doing?"

Preach ran up to him. "They about to race."

"Race? For what? Man, shit I could have stayed home for this shit. Zu nigga what you do?"

They were all pissing me off. "I'm about to do yo bitch if you don't get out of my way."

Chevy still hadn't said a word. Instead, he revved up his bike, building the smoke behind him. Diamond knew shit was real. He moved out of our way. Preach held his hand up, shaking his head. I slid my helmet on. "Chev, we don't even have to do this man," I said in the helmet.

Preach tossed his hand down and Chevy took off.

"Fuck you nigga, ride!"

DIAMOND

When those niggas took off, I hopped on my bike going behind them. I couldn't believe they had got into it. Zu had been running on thin ice, so it was only a matter of time. I sped behind them, getting as close as I could. Chevy was flying down the street. The nigga was cold on the bike. There was no way Zu nor I were going to catch up. I don't know what possessed Zu to even race his ass.

"Y'all niggas need to knock it off!" I yelled.

Zu held up his middle finger in front of me. I sped until I was on the side of him. "Nigga is you dumb?"

"Dumber than a muhfucka," he gritted, speeding off now, turning onto the main street.

Zu was catching up to Chevy as he began going faster, lane switching. "Fuck!"

I tried catching up only to pass Foe, who was coming toward me on the other side of the street. I saw his head turn, but I couldn't focus on him as I tried keeping up. Only a few seconds later I heard him, "Where y'all going?"

"Nigga they racing."

"Who?"

"Chev and Zu!"

Foe took off ahead of me. I was tired. A nigga just got done fucking, and they wanted to race down the street. This time, I sped up. *Car, swerve, car, lean, swerve. Red light.* I ran that bitch. I felt my phone vibrating with the sound of it going off in my headset. "Yo!" I answered.

A giggle filled my ear. "I was calling because I couldn't stop thinking about—"

"Man shit! I'm busy bye," I said, hanging up on her ass.

I knew it would take no time before she began calling, but right now wasn't the time. I had to press pause on Monette's ass. By the time I was close enough, they had turned around to head back. Chevy was hauling ass until his bike went up as if he was doing a wheely, but slammed down to the side, sending him flying. "The fuck!" I shouted.

I rushed over to where he was, hopped off my bike, and ran towards him. "Yo, Chevy!" I hollered.

He still had his helmet on, but he wasn't answering. The guys followed my lead and did the same thing. Getting down on his knees, Zu moved us aside and took off Chevy's helmet. Chevy had lost consciousness. Foe wasted no time calling the paramedics. While I called Preach. For the first time in a long time, I was scared. This was my brother lying here and didn't know what to do.

It took no time for them to arrive. Zu called his little brother Dio to come get Chevy's bike while the rest of us followed behind the paramedics. "What happened?" Preach asked.

"He was riding whooping Zu's ass and boom the nigga fell off the bike."

I could hear Foe huffing and puffing. "Y'all niggas shouldn't have been racing. Probably arguing over something dumb as fuck. Now my nigga down bad," He said as he sped ahead of us.

Zu still hadn't said a word. When we arrived at the hospital, we parked in front of the emergency entrance doors. Security ran up to us, holding out his hand, "Y'all can't park—"

Foe mushed the security right in his face, "Nigga fuck out of here!"

We weren't listening to nobody. All eyes were on us as we entered the emergency room. Four niggas ready to fuck shit up if things with Chevy went bad. Preach went to the front desk, then came over to us as we sat and waited. Zu had his elbow to his knees with his head down. Foe sat there staring off into the distance while Preach stood in front of us. "They said when they have an update someone will come out."

"Fuck that I'm going back there!" Zu shouted.

"Zu man calm yo ass down before they put us out. Right now, isn't the time!" I snapped.

"Fuck was y'all racing for?" Foe jumped in.

I wanted to know too. "I told them to chill. This is what happens when niggas ego's get in the way."

I turned to Zu, "Was this over the race you setup?"

Foe and Preach asked simultaneously. "What race?"

I glanced at both Foe and Preach, then back at Zu. Right then, I knew he hadn't said nothing about it. I held the secret about the race with him and Choppa, but this, I couldn't. Zu's decision making alone was done. If the crew couldn't decide together, then we weren't doing it.

Zu's eyes bounced on all of us. "I told him like I said I would," he paused. "I just hadn't told y'all yet."

"Diamond knows so what is you saying?" Foe jumped in.

"I set up a race with Dragon Heat it's—"

Preach threw his hands up. "If I wasn't a man of God, I swear I would take yo ass to the king. Nigga, we never raced them before. You know they be out there murdering niggas on the pavement. Fuck was you thinking!"

Zu shot up from the seat. "I was thinking about us eating! About us not having to worry about a muhfuckin thing after this race. We all need the money," he gritted.

"You need the money!" Foe snapped.

Zu stopped staring at us. "Man I-I—"

"Where is Chevy!" I heard a female's voice.

We all turned to look at it was the same girl who came to the race and party.

"Harvey?" Zu and Foe said at the same time.

She looked scared as fear struck her badly. "What happened? They called me."

I never realized that Chevy had someone other than us. She had to be extremely close to him if the hospital called her. Nobody knew what to say to her. She walked away from us and straight to the front desk while Zu was on her heels. "They fucking?" I pointed.

"Diamond nigga not right now dawg," Preach chimed in.

Zu tried touching her, and she pulled away. I saw the nurse open the door for her and she went into the back, leaving Zu standing there. I never seen him chase after a girl before. My phone vibrated again, and I saw it was Monette. I was going to hit the ignore button on her, but I answered.

"What's good?"

"Why did you hang up on me? Is everything OK?"

I really wasn't up for the small talk. She was still sitting high on my shits list. "Mo what's up? You keep calling so what is it I can do you for?"

"Damn like that?"

"We had a deal I took you out, put a little dick in you so that case you have on my grandma should be closed by morning."

The phone fell silent. "You know what you're right, I don't even know why I bothered. Bye."

Monette hung up, and frankly, I didn't care. Right now, the focus was on Chevy. I would hit her when I was ready.

HARVEY

It wasn't long after Foe dropped me off that the hospital called me, informing me that I was listed as a point of contact for Chevy. I didn't even let them finish talking before I hopped in my car, taking off to get there. When I arrived and saw all the guys there, a part of my heart felt warm because Chevy had brothers to be there for him. However, when I saw Zu, I became annoyed that I even let him suck me into dumbass world of drama. The type of dick he served explained all I needed to know. Tonight, I didn't want to be bothered any further with him.

When the nurse walked me back to where Chev was, my feet felt heavy. The cold halls, the smell of latex gloves and the sounds dinging coming from rooms signally the patient needed help made my stomach curl. When we reached the room, she stopped me. "He's awake very angry but hopefully you can get him to calm down some."

I nodded as I entered the room. Chev was lying there, staring at the TV with no sound. He cut his eyes at me, then back at the TV. "Chev!" I called out.

"I'm good, you can leave," he muttered.

He knew damn well I wasn't going anywhere. He was my brother and the love I had for him was unconditional. I didn't care how much he demanded for me to leave; he knew I wasn't going anywhere. I stepped over to his bedside, looking down at him. "What happened?"

Chevy's eye raised, but they weren't the same. It was something different about them this time. Although he would never admit it, he was terrified. Something was wrong, and I wanted to know and know now. I held his hand. "What is it?"

He adjusted himself on the bed. "I was dehydrated, and a nigga passed out." He shrugged.

I turned up my face. "You're lying because all you do is drink water, fresh fruit juice and take all those holistic vitamins and shit. Next."

"Well, they ain't working."

"Of all people you shouldn't be afraid to tell me. We been through way too much shit for you to act like this June," I said to him.

I knew that would trigger him, but I wanted answers. He picked up the remote, turning the TV off. "Go grab a chair," he instructed me.

I went to the reclining chair pushing it toward him, "Nigga of all things yo simple ass get that."

I started laughing. "What shit, I want to be comfortable."

Once I sat down, he turned slightly toward me. "What happened between you and Zu?"

I knew he's been dying to ask me, but I didn't want to share that with him because what if it messed up the friendship he and Zu had? I didn't want to be the reason they got into it. "Did you sleep with Lola?" I responded.

"No."

"She said—"

"What did I say? This dick is elite I don't just fuck anybody."

My face balled up. "Well okay then." I laughed. "You need a girlfriend maybe then yo ass won't be so grumpy."

He nodded his head. "You need to find a better nigga to fuck with."

I sat Indian style in the chair as I leaned forward. "Chev I can make my own decision about who I want to mess with. Sometimes my choice may not be the ones you approve of, but I have to learn and go through it myself. I appreciate you being there for me but for once you need to find someone for you. Now tell me what's wrong."

He ran his hand over his waves, then leaned back, staring at the wall ahead. "I need to get to Toussaint. I'm good just need some rest is all and like you said I have to learn and go through it myself."

Just like that, he would not talk about it anymore. Chevy had been through everything alone. It was like when one of his foster parents would lock him in the closet for hours without food, and when he ate, it would be unhealthy scraps. It was a reason for him being as mindful as he was about food. Or how he was alone when a different foster family who already had their own children would exclude him from things. Chevy's past made him who is now and a part of that was not opening up.

I grabbed the remote from his bed turning the TV back on, "I'm going to go get the guys their out there shaking in their boots so let's put them at ease by bringing them back here. They want to support you as well," I explained.

"Them niggas scared," he joked, but didn't smile.

I got up from the chair heading to the door, "Harvey, I will handle Triece, you just be careful with Zu. I don't want to have to put a bullet in my nigga."

I walked out of the room, going to get the guys. When I came out of the entrance, they all stood. Before I could even tell them to come back, they walked over to me. The security walked over, pointing at them, "Only two at a time," he hissed.

"Nigga please!" Foe spat.

They all followed behind me toward the room. If only Chevy could see the type of support he had, I'm sure it would make him feel much better. I slowed down, walking to let them go ahead of me after showing them which room it was. Zu came up to me, sliding his fingers between mine. "A nigga sorry, can we start over?" he whispered.

This I wasn't expecting, but it made me smile. I trusted Chevy's words, so I looked at Zu and told him yes.

"Can a nigga take you out?"

"Yes."

He leaned forward, planting a kiss on my neck. "You Zu baby now."

He and I both went into the room with everyone else. Although he apologized, I just hope like hell he wouldn't make me regret my decision to give him another chance.

Chapter Six

ZU
Bad Habits

It had been two days, and they were finally releasing Chevy. Harvey told me not to ask what was going on with him, but she didn't need to tell me that because I knew he wouldn't share it. I'd just hoped whatever it was, my nigga would be good. I figured once he was feeling better; I needed to tell him about me putting up the Juice bar. I honestly wish I could cancel the race, but shit wasn't that easy.

Since Harvey said she had to work today, I picked my nigga up from the hospital. By the time I pulled up, he was waiting outside. I hopped out to open the door for him, but of course, his grumpy ass stood there. "What nigga you gone get in?"

Chevy's eyes followed me, "I ain't no bitch I can open the door nigga I still got use of my limbs."

We got in and I took off. For the first few minutes, everything was silent. I knew I should have talked him out of racing, but our pride was in the way. We both were trying to prove a point and still got nowhere. I cleared my throat before speaking. "Look, I want to apologize. I didn't mean for shit to happen the way they did," I started.

"Shit cool, you just make sure you treat Harvey like you supposed to. She ain't Triece."

I had been meaning to ask him if he and Harvey ever fucked because he was so protective over her. Hell, we didn't even know about her until recently. I turned the radio down some. "Let me ask you something," I paused. "You and Harvey y'all ever—"

His head swiveled my way. "You fucked already so what does it matter? But nah, never she's sister. Harvey and I been through rough times together and she's the only one who understands me. So again, tread lightly nigga."

I let out a light exhale. I didn't want to have to drop her ass because she and my nigga had something. I wasn't too far from his crib before he started rambling, "She love surprises, hate going to the movies, enjoy flowers if their given to her at the right time and she a hopeless romantic."

"Damn nigga you sure you—"

He cut his eyes at me. "No, that's my word. See the difference between me and you I pay attention to what women like, their needs, what makes them smile. I like to feed their mind and soul then I fuck them it makes the experience better and the pussy," he shook his head. "The pussy is wetter than the ocean floor. I like the connection. If I'm with a woman our soul got to connect. You just like to fuck."

I started cracking up because this nigga was wild. This was coming from a man who we rarely seen with any female. It made sense though, because Chev was particular. He picked his women like picking out the finest wine. It wasn't so much about how it looked on the outside, but about the taste, how long it had been preserving, and the delicacy. The nigga had game. It was just the wall he built around himself that was holding him back.

I wanted to take what he told me about Harvey and apply it, but my way because I was still a hood nigga. I wasn't the soft fluffy type, but for Harvey, I would try. It was something about her that made me want to really get to know her. I had now pulled up to his crib. Before I could kill the engine, he stopped me. "I'm good. Let's link up tomorrow tell them niggas to be there on time. We got some shit to talk about," he said, then got out of the car.

I watched Chevy as he strolled up to his crib. My brother was really going through something, and nobody knew what the fuck it was. We all needed to put in to help him with whatever it was it. Chevy was the glue to Zoo, and that's on everything.

I took off, heading to Harvey. I'd made a few stops before arriving at her job. The area she worked in was more uppity than where Chevy lived. As I stepped inside the building, I could see the women from each little studio I passed poking their heads out of their sliding door. "Damn he fine!" I heard someone yell.

A nigga was flattered but my mind was on one person only, Harvey. Before I could reach her suite, an older lady stepped in front of me. "You sure are a handsome, thick, tall man."

I smiled. "Thank you, ma'am."

She tapped my arm, "Aw you don't," she paused, squeezing my arm, "Damn!"

I could tell they weren't getting broke off like they should. I continued to walk until I reached her suite. I didn't even knock, I just walked in. "Zu!" she screamed.

"Shit! Girl that's you?" a girl sitting in the chair across from her said.

Harvey's eyes looked me up and down. "She asked you a ✤ question."

She smiled, then glanced at the girl, "I'm thinking about it."

"My ass. Man, stop playing," I told her as I walked up to her, squeezing her cheeks, turning her head my way, sticking my tongue in her mouth.

Just like I thought, she sucked on that muhfucka too. "Exactly!"

I waited while she finished the girl's nails. I was getting annoyed because of the uncomfortable chair I was sitting in.

"Man is you done?" I blurted out.

Harvey's head spun, "Zu!"

"This shit is uncomfortable, small ass room. I'm about to get yo own spot. This shit small as fuck. Them claws ain't done yet," I said, trying to look over her shoulders.

I could hear the girl sucking her teeth.

"My bad."

About another thirty minutes passed before Harvey was done. She cleaned up, and we headed out. She strolled toward her car, but I stopped her. "Where you going?"

"To my car, I can't leave it."

I grabbed her by her shirt, picking her up tossing her over my shoulder. "Man, I waited all fucking day you coming with me."

"Put me down!" she yelled.

When I got to my ride, I put her down, then opened the door for her. She went to get in, then stopped. "Zu!" she squealed.

Flowers, perfume, five bands, and a big ass gorilla stuff animal. The look on her face was priceless. Maybe Chevy was on to something. Seeing her so happy for something I considered small made a nigga feel mushy inside. It made me want to do it more often. Harvey took a good grip of my shirt, pulling me down and kissing me. "Better stop before I fuck you in this parking lot," I mumbled between kisses.

"I'm not scared. Are you?"

Was she challenging me? "Zu never scared baby. She'll get ate, let me take you out first, let a nigga try to be a gentleman," I told her.

She smiled. We got in and sped off. I didn't know what the cards held for Harvey and me, but as of now, I liked this hand.

DIAMOND

"Nights like this I wish raindrops would fall-ah-all," I sang as we waited around for Chevy to arrive.

Foe threw something at me. "Nigga shut up! Ole Rico suave ass nigga," he laughed.

Zu walked over to us. "I think we need to do something for Chevy."

Preach pulled his eyes away from what he was looking at, focusing on Zu. "Like what?"

"Like a party or something. My nigga going through it. I want to show our appreciation for him."

"I'm with it." Foe chimed in.

Preach came closer to us, "Zoo day is coming up why don't we do it then?"

Zu waved his hand. "Nah I want to do it before then. Zoo day is too hectic, I want the attention and focus to be on him. Especially with this race coming up I need him in good spirits."

"Why?" I had now jumped in.

We all focused in on him because we knew bullshit was coming next. "Because he's the one that's racing."

"Hell nah!" we all screamed in unison.

Foe shot up, pointing to Zu, "Fuck no! the nigga almost died riding. You think we letting him get on a bike, especially to race? Hell, do the nigga even know he the one racing?"

"Who racing?" Chevy voice pierced are ears.

This nigga always showed up on point. We all looked at Zu since it was all his idea we wanted him to explain.

He turned to Chevy, "You, my nigga I put you up to race."

It was in this moment I think all of us were holding our breath.

"Aight," he calmly said.

Foe rushed over to Chevy, "Nigga you sick? Fuck you mean. Yo ass was almost on a shirt and you talking about aight."

"I'm good. Zu know what it is," Chevy replied, removing his jacket. "See what Zu ain't tell y'all is if we lose, I'm out, I'm stepping away from Zoo."

He began moving between us. "I love Zoo, remember Zoo over everything, but I have things I got to do and it's only fair I explore those things."

Preach move toward Zu, "Fuck, is he talkin' about?

Zu stood there, jaws clenching. He had really fucked up with this one. Normally I would be quick to make a joke, but

109

Chevy wanting to leave the crew wasn't nothing to joke about. Him leaving means Zu would more than likely pull in the races and so far, his decisions have been ass. "Chevy you can't leave the crew," I said to him.

He walked over to the bar, grabbed the jar of weed, and began rolling him a blunt. "I can do what I want. I showed you niggas a lot, y'all will be good. Zu got it, right Zu?" he stopped, looked at Zu then continued. "A little birdy told me that my business," he halted now, walking up to Zu. "My baby, my first fucking business," he clapped his hands together in rage. "Something I put you on too," he slapped Zu's chest with the back of his hand. "Has been put as collateral for this fuckin race."

I knew this was bound to happen. "I told yo ass!" I blurted out.

Chevy head swung my way, "Wait so you knew and you ain't say shit!" he barked.

I felt bad as hell, "Chev I—"

"Fuck that! It took a lot for me to get that shit going. Hungry nights, being homeless, robbing peter to pay paul bitch ass and this how y'all do me? You know what, fuck the race once it's over I'm out!" he roared, snatching up his jacket and leaving.

We all stood there. I looked at Zu and shook my head. "Nigga I don't know what the fuck you got to do but you need to fix this shit," I told him.

"You got a lot of begging to do from God cause ain't no way yo ass this dumb," Preach said as he left after Chevy.

I didn't have words as I headed out too. I prayed God would fix this because honestly Zoo was the only family I had outside of my grandma and hanging with her ass every day wasn't it.

I'd finally called up Monette after blowing her off for the last week or so. She and I would text here and there, but nothing more than a simple conversation. I found it funny that I never received paperwork for my grandma on the case she claimed she had on her. I ended up calling to find out the shit never existed. *Strike one.* She had been on my radar super heavy, but I liked her.

Today I wanted to take her out to see where her head was at. This would determine if I would really move forward with her or leave it where it was. Maybe her reason for doing what she did was because she wanted to be close to me.

As I was pulling up to her apartment, I spotted Nash and a few of his boys leaving the building. I didn't think nothing of it as I parked, as they sped off on their bikes. Upon reaching her door, I knocked a few times. When she answered. She responded with wide, surprised eyes. "What are you doing here?"

"Don't ask questions, go get dress were going out," I told her.

She stepped aside, letting me in. I enjoyed Mo in her natural state. It was nothing like looking at her fresh face. "Make yourself comfortable it won't take me long," she said as she disappeared into the back.

I glanced around her crib and notice a picture of her and a small child. Then another photo of her and a familiar face. About ten minutes later, she stepped into the living room. "I'm ready."

I smiled. "I see you learning," I told her.

She wore a pair of jeans that capture every curve she had and an orange crop top. "Yeah, won't be no hiking up a dress today." She giggled.

I pointed at the picture, "Who's the kid?"

She got quiet as she glanced at it. I could see that it meant a lot to her, whoever it was. "That's my little brother. It's an old picture he was seven in that now he's eighteen," she softly spoke.

"Where is he?"

"I don't know. That was the last time I saw him and after that he was taken from my mother. I've been looking for him ever since."

Shit reminded me of Chevy. "I can talk to my boy and see if we can find him," I told her, reaching out for her hand.

I could see her getting emotional and I wasn't trying to do that, but I never had siblings. I was an only child, but if I did, I wouldn't stop until I found them. "It's all good when it's time for us to meet again we will."

"And the lady in the other picture?"

"Unfortunately, that's my mother."

Her mom was a Sherm head. She always came to our annual carwash day. Chevy would hook her up with food and shit. I chose not to bring it up because I didn't want to mess up the moment. We headed out, hopped on my bike, and left. The ride was silent. I could hear her sniffles in my ear. I wanted to say something, but I figured she just wanted to be left alone while she reminisced. When I pulled up to the spot, I could hear her giggle. "Karaoke Diamond really?"

"Yeah, unless you got something else in mind?"

She didn't object. We headed inside. The bar was packed. I held her hand as we squeezed through the crowd to the small section I booked for us. When the waitress came over, I ordered two bottles of champagne. Monette's eyes lit up as she watched the girl on stage, slurring her words and singing. I wanted to ask her about the shit with my grandma, but I needed to get her comfortable first. "Thank you," she said, looking at me and smiling.

"For what?"

She placed her hands on my lap. "For taking me out. For making me smile. Before I met you," she looked down, then back at me. "My life was miserable. I still have my days, but you seem to make it better somehow."

Fingers to her chin. "You special Mo. I just hope you know a nigga like me don't do shit like this, so I hope you don't fuck me over," I winked.

The waitress had now come with the bottles. I poured us up, and we drank, shooting the shit for a bit until a song came on that was clearly her favorite. She jumped up and start shaking her ass. She took my hand, making me stand up while she bent over and started grinding all over me. I held the bottle up, moving along with her. Mo's movements in the dimly lit corner, illuminated by the strobe light, were mesmerizing. She stood straight, leaning her back against my chest. Our lips were so close, all we could do was kiss. "Soft ass lips," I muttered in her mouth.

I slid my hand down her stomach and into her tight jeans. She undid the button on them, allowing me more access. I ran my hand over her smooth pussy. My lips sucking on her neck while we rocked to the music, and I played with her pussy. She reached back, taking the back of my head in her hands, pulling my face toward her lips. We sucked on each other while my fingers went to work. I stroked her so good she came all over my fingers.

Mo was doing something to me. I tried falling for women before being really into them, but all they wanted to do was to be tied to Zoo. They wanted the exposure. She wasn't like that, but I still didn't fully trust her yet. I'd stepped away to go wash my hands. I was only gone for a few minutes. As I approached my section, I saw a nigga in her face and it ticked me off. *Strike two.* I rushed over there. I shoved his ass. "Nigga who the fuck are you?" he gritted.

I held the two fingers up that were just playing between Mo's legs. "The nigga that just finger fuck that pussy!"

Maybe I should have asked questions. Instead, I grabbed the bottle we were just sipping on, busting the nigga's shit wide open. "Ole washed up ass nigga!" I barked.

Mo threw her hand over her mouth. "Diamond!"

Whap! Whap!

I began pounding on his ass. "Big butter bean head ass nigga. Fuck you in her face for!"

Whap!

He picked me up, tossing my ass, sending my body into the wall. I staggered to get up. That only set me off more. I rushed his ass, sending his big ass up, slamming him on his back.

Whap! Whap!

My fist to his face was becoming endless. One of his boys came up. I guess the goal was to beat my ass, but I was ready for whatever. If that meant turning this bitch inside out by myself, I was ready. I heard Foe's voice. "Bitch nigga it's Zoo! I'm about to noodle yo shit!"

I looked up to see him holding the burner to the nigga's side. That's when more dudes stepped up. "It's about to get real rowdy in this muthfucka." Zu said as he and Preach stepped up. Next thing I know, a bottle flew into my section damn near hitting Foe and he lost it. He hopped over the rails, diving like he was crowd surfing.

After that, we all started fighting. Zu was pounding on another nigga and I was hitting any nigga who stepped up, knocking their ass back.

A nigga pulled his gun out on Preach. "It would be in your best interest to put that shit up," I heard Preach say.

"What you gone do if I don't!" The nigga barked at Preach.

He flicked his nose, turning to face the guy. "Every day I pray I don't have to backslide and everyday a nigga tries me. He who findeth a Glock in my face findeth one in theirs," he gritted as he quickly whipped out, aiming his gun at the dude.

"Nigga fuck—"

Whap!

Preach hit the nigga with the butt of the gun and went to work on his ass. Security came rushing over, dragging us out

116

of the club. Mo was right behind me with both helmets and my jacket.

She tried touching me but moved her away. "It wasn't that serious."

"Yes, the fuck it was. How you know that nigga and before you lie yet again, I'm not in the fucking mood!"

Confusion sat on her face. "You know what, don't even."

I walked over to my boys, telling them I was good. I snatched my helmet from her. "Get the fuck on the bike so I can take you home."

"No, why are you acting like this?"

"Mo get on the bike!"

"No!"

I didn't have time for her playing dumb. I snatched the other helmet from her and started my shit up and took off. I was pressing pause on her ass until I felt otherwise. I knew I really liked her because I had gotten out of character, but my instincts were telling me I needed to really leave her ass alone. So, for now, that's what I was going to do.

FOE

We had about two weeks before the race with Dragon Heat, and Zu still hadn't made shit right with Chevy. We had set up a little get together to get Zu and Chevy back talking again. There was no way we were going to win a race when none of our heads or hearts were in it. The brotherhood we had felt like it was deteriorating slowly, and I wasn't feeling it. I hoped like hell Chevy showed up on the day of his party so we could rectify the situation.

To get my mind off things, I called up Asia. I wanted to be on some chill shit and being in her presence seemed like the fix for it. She'd text me her address and when I saw it, I knew shorty probably had a story to tell. Asia lived in the projects. One of the grimiest ones at that. I was familiar because it was the same ones I did a lot of my dirt in when I was heavy in the streets. She must have been new to these because I'd never seen her before. I knew almost everyone out there.

When I pulled up, the first person I saw was Zu's brother Dio with a bunch of fucks niggas. When he spotted me, he came dapping me up. "What's good my G?"

I glanced over his shoulders at the little niggas he was hanging with, then back at him. "Zu gone beat yo ass you hanging out here."

He waved me off. "Man, Zeus ain't gone do shit," he laughed. "I'm good. Who you here for? Tryna get some gas?"

"I don't fuck with project weed, shit probably laced. Get yo ass out of here. Fuck them niggas they ain't putting no money in yo pockets."

He slowly nodded his head. "I hear you my G," he said as he walked back over to his friends.

Dio reminded me of how hardheaded I was until Chevy saved me from the streets. We all had bad habits. The key was whether or not we would break them. Moments later, Asia came strolling down the walkway to my bike. Her short ass was swaying those hips. Her wide smile exposed her teeth. *She's so pretty.* I thought to myself. I handed her a helmet as she got on behind me. Before taking off, I could hear Dio and his friends yelling. "We only fuck with da Zoo!"

Asia's laugh filled my ears. "Let's do something chill. Can we go back to your place?" she asked.

It seemed as if we were thinking alike. I'd never really brought women to the crib. Preach and I shared a condo, and we were always cautious about who we would bring around. However, I fucked with little shorty, so I headed back to my place. When I pulled up, I notice Preach wasn't there, which was cool. Knowing him, he was probably out doing some church shit with his pops. I could see Asia's eyes bouncing all over my spot as she walked in. Before her ass could touch the carpet, I stopped her. "Hold on mama, shoes off."

She smacked her lips, looking at me like I was joking. "My spot my rules. What yo feet crunch or something? Them bitches got corns. Cause I don't do ugly ass feet."

She burst into laughter, giving me the middle finger. "I keep my shit done," she said as she slid her shoes off.

My eyes quickly moved down to her feet. They were pretty as hell. Cute small toes with yellow polish. "Yeah, what you got to say now?"

I held both hands up as I stepped back, "You got it mama."

I directed her to my room and first thing she did was get on my bed. I almost lost my shit. "Get yo ass up. If you want to get on my bed fine, but them clothes got to come off," I grumbled.

She put her hands on her hips, "Really Foe?"

"Nigga yes really. If you lived like I did you would understand why. I grew up in dirty ass homes. Even when I tried keeping my space clean, too many kids around fuck that up. Living with roaches, limited food, and six kids with one bathroom. Baby, I need a clean space for a clear head."

By the time I was done with what I said, she was down to her panties and bra. Although Asia was slim, her body was nice. A small pair of hips, apple booty, and small titties. Small waist, cute face. She held a scar on her stomach. "What happened?" I asked, running my finger across it.

She shrugged. "A nigga attacked me one night. He raped me."

The way she carried it was like she didn't care, but hearing shit like that fueled me. I had sisters and if it even crossed a nigga's mind, it's one to the temple with no shame. Asia placed her hand to my face. "I learned to deal with it. It's my burden not yours. I'm good, though."

I took her hand, leading her to the bathroom. I came out of my shirt and pants. I grabbed my gun, giving it to her. "Look in the mirror," I told her.

She did as I instructed. I got behind, pressing my chest to her back. Asia's soft skin to mine only made my dick hard, but I needed to focus because what I was doing was not to fuck her, but to show her something. "Hold that shit up," I whispered in her ear.

She looked in the mirror and our eyes burned into each other. Mama lived a rough life. I could see it. She held a tinge of pain in her eyes and so did I. My forty-five set nicely in her hands as she aimed it at the mirror. I brought my hands up, resting under hers. "As long as you got this a nigga better never touch you like that again. As long as you got this you are safe. As—"

"But I don't have you," she mumbled.

I kissed the side of her face, then glanced back at her in the mirror. "You are beautiful, you are smart, you are mine," I told her.

She sat the gun down and turned around, wrapping her arms around my neck. I accepted it by wrapping my arms around her waist, picking her up and placing her on the sink's edge. "Stay right here."

I walked out to grab something and came back. When she saw what was in my hand, she laughed, but I didn't. I slid the pooh shiesty mask over her face. Then I put one over mine. "This some hood nigga shit," she uttered.

"Yeah, and I'm yo hood nigga. Sexy ass."

I kissed her. I kissed her passionately through the opening of the mask. She placed both hands to the side of my face to bring me in closer. I closed the space between us. I unlatched her bra, easing it off. My tongue glided over her collarbone, down the center of her chest. I took one of her nipples in my mouth, letting my tongue tap dance over it. Asia's breathing picked up. "Mm," she softly moaned.

I picked her up, walking her to my bed, lying her down. I kissed her stomach. Kissed her scar. I didn't know if what and me and her were doing was going to take any of the pain away she was harboring, but I was going to do my best to fuck some of it away. See, what Asia didn't know is that I was a protector. I wanted to protect anyone I cared for. Now that she had come into my life, I had placed her on that list. We were about to give ourselves to each other and once we finished, Asia belonged to me. It would be my job going forward to make sure shorty was good.

I used only my teeth pulling her panties off. Her head shot up, "Foe, you sure you want to do this?"

"Yes, mama a nigga sure."

I kissed her inner thighs, gripping them, pulling her to the edge of the bed. She lifted, looking at me. "Let's take the masks off," she whispered.

I held my hand out, "Chill mama you good. I'm going to fuck you with it on." I smiled.

I grabbed a condom from the draw and slid it on. I sat next to her on the bed, tapping my lap. Asia wasted no time getting on top of me. Both her hands to my shoulders as she rode me. She began rocking back and forth, rolling her hips. It was as if she was dancing but riding dick. Her pussy felt crazy, had my head spinning. Her palm gripped the back of my neck as she brought her forehead to mine. "I like this hood dick."

"Keep fuckin' riding so I can show you how hood I can be."

I flipped her ass over, putting both her legs to her head. I heard her ass grunt a little, but with me she was going to have to learn to take this dick. I locked my arms between her legs, tighten my grip around her ankles.

"Mm, mama," I moaned.

Asia's mouth was open. She looked like she couldn't breathe.

"You good?"

"Mm hmm, keep fucking me like this," she whined.

I placed one leg to the bed and let my hips do its thing. I was pounding Asia's pussy so hard it was the only thing you heard in the room. She went from moaning to grunting, but she was taking it, all of it. "You take dick so good mama," I growled.

"Foe oh my God!" she cried.

"Nah, God ain't got nothing to do with this. Say something else."

"Fuck!" she went into vibrato.

Shit was so good, had me saying anything. "Sexy ass. Hood ass. Fire ass pussy."

With the work I was putting in, she would sure be sore in the morning. I'd finally release my arms, allowing her to wrap her legs around my waist. Asia then spun me, and I was on my back. She got on top in reverse. She bounced her ass almost perfectly. She went up to the tip, then slammed down. "*Goddamn!*" I grunted.

"Yeah, now what nigga?"

I lifted her back to my chest. I gripped the back of her neck and moved at the same pace as her. Before you know it, we had both cum together. We laid in the bed and rolled a few blunts until she had dosed off.

I watched her as she slept. The truth is, I was afraid to bring a woman in my life, especially when my attention was focus on other shit. I didn't know if Asia was good for me, but I was just going to let the chips fall where they fall. What I didn't need was a need bad habit I couldn't shake.

Chapter Seven

MONETTE
Bitches Vs Zoo

It had been a week since I've talked to Diamond. I figured by now he would have at least picked up the phone to call me, but he hadn't. I was pissed at first, but now I was dying to see him. I didn't understand why he got so upset Nash's homeboy came up to me, telling Nash had been trying to reach me and he wanted to meet up. I was trying to get him out of the section, but before I could, Diamond came up so fast, causing crazy ass havoc. It was sudden, chaotic, risky and a fucking turn on. I'd never had a man so possessive over me.

My intention was to tell him about Nash's plan, but I felt he and I were making a connection, and I didn't want to ruin it. I was falling for Diamond and the last thing I wanted to do was hurt him.

Now here I was waiting for Nash to show up to this place he had me meet him at and he was taking forever. I just wanted to tell him I would pay him back, even if it meant I had to pay him weekly. I wanted to be done. Besides the way Diamond was moving, I would not get too much information out of him, anyway. I was about to drive off when light taps on my window caused me to look. It was Nash and another girl. I didn't know who she was, but my gut was telling me this shit was only about to get worse. I hit the locks, allowing them both to get in. I didn't waste no time. "Who the fuck is she?"

I heard her smack her lips. "First off, calm yo ass down. She's the other part to my plan. The secret to getting to them niggas is bitches. I just need y'all to find out if they have any races coming up if so, how much on the table and where the fuck they are hiding all the guns. After that I'll do the rest. So, if y'all need to throw some pussy then do so. Monette, I want you to hit Chevy's ass."

Nash was out of his mind. It was too late for me to fuck with whoever this Chevy was because Diamond and I had already been intimate.

"Clarence was not worth all this."

"Clarence was! That nigga owes bread and he didn't come through and they tryna make me pay. If I'm going to pay, it's coming from the Zoo. Besides Clarence is yo fuckin cousin you should be mad about it too. I know them niggas did it!"

To me, Clarence was a low budget hustler who tried to hustle anyone, even his own momma, so no I didn't feel sad about it. I didn't even know why I entertained it. "Who is Chevy?"

"Oh, he's that nigga in them streets. I heard don't nobody fuck with him either," the girl in the back seat said.

"Who are you?"

"Oh, I'm Simone," she smiled.

Simone was gorgeous. I couldn't believe Nash brought her into this. "Why are you doing this?"

"Enough with the questions."

"No! I can ask. I'm waiting."

She looked at Nash, then back at me. "I'm just trying to be a part of the Knights, Nash said if I can get him something he'll put me on."

I rolled my eyes. "You could have fucked him for that. Girl if you know like I do you'll walk away. It ain't worth it."

"Then why you doing it?"

Nash slammed his hand on the console. "Shut yo ass up! Now, like I said, either you help me, or someone is going to come see you and that business will be gone. They don't like people who fraud the government. Acting like a case worker all in them people's homes."

"Get out!" I shouted.

Nash got out and Simone stayed in. "I really like Preach and I don't want to do this. Your cousin is crazy, but the Zoo Boyz are crazier and if Nash knew what was good for him, he might want to back out now. I'm trying to find a way out, but Nash has something on me, and it can't come out. Just know I'm going to do whatever it takes to get myself out of this," she said as she got out of the car.

Something about what Simone said didn't sit right with me. *Shit!* I was in a bind and didn't know how I was going to get out of this. If I informed Diamond about the situation, it would not only ignite a war, but Diamond would hate me and never talk to me again. Then Nash would find a way to ruin me. If I chose not to reveal it, I would still face destruction.

I drove off, heading to Diamond's. Despite having a million things going through my head, I wanted to see him. I almost felt thirsty at this point because what he served me the other night, I wanted it again and I wanted it now. When I arrived at his building, I called him.

I wasn't expecting him to answer, but he did. "What's up Mo?"

The way he sounded had me smiling ear to ear. "Diamond, I was in the area trying to see what you were up to if you wanted to chill?"

"Come up Mo," he said dryly.

I didn't like how he was acting. Although I was plotting against him, he didn't know it, so why was he treating me this way? He acted like the man in the bar was touching me. I pulled in the parking garage parking in the first spot I saw. I took the elevator up to his floor. As soon as the doors slid open, he was standing right there. He looked good as hell.

"Come on I want to take you somewhere," he said as he pressed the button for the elevator to go back down. When we got back to the parking garage, he hit an alarm.

"You have a car?"

Diamond laughed loudly, making me feel dumb. "I don't know what kind of niggas you been fucking with, but it's obvious they some lame ones," he finished as he opened the door to white beamer allowing me to slide in.

I just knew he was going to talk about what happened at the bar, but he didn't. Diamond drove through downtown like he owned it while I sat next to him feeling like a passenger Princess. He glanced over at me, then tapped my chin with his finger. "How was your day? You look good by the way."

He had this aura about him that was demanding, but smooth. His smile would put you in a good mood, even if you didn't want to be. He had become a surprise in my life, and it was the only beginning. I thought about telling him what was going with Nash, but I didn't want to fuck up the mood or my dick appointment. Instead, I sat back and enjoyed the ride. When we finally stopped. The lounge we were at had tinted windows that prevented you from seeing inside.

He helped me out of the car before valet took it away. As we stepped in, the music was the first that caught my attention.

130

A cute little R&B mix. To the left along the entire wall were plush orange couches and brown marble looking tables with Hookahs on each one. There was a bar to the right, a small stage sitting toward the back of the lounge, and a small dance floor.

"This place is nice. I like the vibe," I told him as I grabbed his hand. "If I would have known you were bringing me here, I would have dressed up more."

Diamond squeezed my hand. "It's all good Mo' you look fine, besides this my spot. Didn't you read the sign before walking in?"

I didn't. I didn't care to because I was in Diamond land, and I didn't give two shits about what was going on around me. That's when I saw the orange glow sign above the bar that clearly said Diamonds. He walked me over to one couch in a dimly lit corner. Once we sat down, he began setting up the hookah. There were a few people inside mingling, but I'm sure in a few hours this place would be packed.

Moments later, a waitress brought over a bottle, giving it to him. The way she looked at him, I wondered if she fucked him before. A tinge of jealously struck me. I leaned over, planting a tongue fuck to his neck. She rolled her eyes and walked away. Diamond leaned to the side. "No need for all that Mo, she works for me you would know if I hit that."

"What is that supposed to mean?"

Fingers to my chin. "It means I would never bring you around someone I fuck with before. It's not my style, now chill," he said, then kissed me on my cheek.

I didn't want a measly ass peck on the cheek. I wanted him to stick his tongue in my mouth, then between my legs. It had been a while since I've been with a man and this one; I wanted bad. Each time he touched me, I craved him more. He opened the bottle and put it in front of me.

"I know you a lady and shit but with me we do whatever the fuck we want, now open yo mouth."

I didn't hesitate. I opened wide, allowing him to pour the drink down my throat.

"My nigga Diamond!" I heard someone call out.

When my head came forward, I saw one of friends from his crew. "Zu!"

Zu? Maybe he was the leader of the crew, but Nash said Chevy. I thought. They did some type of handshake. He was with a girl that I saw at the party, but she wasn't the one in his face. They both glanced at me, and I gave a shy wave. Diamond place his hand to the small of my back as he introduced me, "This is Mo, Monette. That's Zu my brother and his shorty Harvey."

"I'm his friend, not his girl."

"As long as we fucking you my girl," Zu jumped in.

"I know that's right," I smiled.

They walked over to the far end of the couches sitting down. I was tired of waiting. I leaned over to Diamond, who was bobbing his head to the music while drinking from the bottle.

"I want to fuck."

His gaze fell on me. "Shit what's up then?"

"Let's go."

"Nah Mo you want to fuck let's fuck. Can't nobody see us in the corner."

My eyes scanned around. Although we were in the corner, I felt like everyone could see us. "But Diamond."

He shook his head. "Then you don't want to fuck. You can't be acting scary around me," he said seriously.

I didn't know if I could fuck this man right here. Maybe I didn't want it that badly. I sat back, folding my arms over my chest, mad as hell.

FOE

"All you got to do is hold it like this, keep your arms straight and focus on your target when your ready fire that bitch," I directed Asia.

"Like this?"

"Yup mama just like that."

Bloaw! Bloaw!

Her small frame bucked back twice. She turned to me, smirking. I hit the button on the belt, bringing the target forward. Little shorty ate, hitting the red dot precisely. I was skeptical on bringing Asia here because most girls like to go to dinner or movies, but going to the gun range on a date wasn't their first choice.

Asia sat the gun down, now stepping in front of me. "I told you I'm a shoota," she said, doing the gun motion at me.

I nodded my head, "I see you; I see you."

Preach came over to me, "Ya'll ready to shake?"

I looked at Asia, "You ready?"

She nodded her head. "This was so much fun!" Simone poked her head from the other side of the wall.

Preach and I did a double date since he had been talking to Simone since the night we went to her house. It surprised me because again, he never gave women a chance. He said he wanted to know what she was up to because he didn't trust her, so maybe this was his way of finding out. We headed out, hopping in separate cars, and headed to our next destination.

"Foe, you a real vibe you know that?"

I glanced at her, "I just be chilling. What else you into beside fucking me?" I asked her.

"Smoking, chilling and reading."

"So, you're an introvert?"

She started laughing. "What you know about it?"

"What you mean? Just because I'm a street nigga don't mean I don't know shit. I'm that nigga mama."

Asia's smile was bright. I continued to drive until we reached the lounge. As soon as I opened the door for Asia, some random nigga walked up to her. "Spicy! Girl is that you?"

I cut my eyes as Asia, and she looked away. "Fuck is he talkin' about Spicy?"

He stepped between us, "Girl I've been looking for you. Why ain't been at the club."

I shoved that nigga so hard he flew into the nearest wall. "Nigga don't be walking up on her like that fuck is wrong with you," I gritted.

I turned to Asia, "Fuck is he talkin' about?"

The nigga came back, and I whipped out on his ass, "Nigga, you better fall the fuck back, or them ankles gone be sitting curbside."

Asia ran in front of the gun. "Foe chill, I'm a stripper. I dance."

I lowered my gun, peering at her, "You shaking yo ass in the club? Why you ain't say that when I just asked what you were into?"

"I didn't want you to judge me."

Preach and Simone had now walked up. "You good over there?" Preach asked.

"Always."

He walked inside, with Simone behind him. The guy stood there, "My bad Spicy I'm—"

I swung, *Whap!* "I just told yo ass!" I barked.

Whap!

I grabbed Asia's hand, dragging her in the building. I passed by everybody, taking her straight to the back. I went into the Diamon's office, slamming the door behind me. "Damn, it's not that serious."

"If it's not, why you didn't say nothing about it. If you dance, you dance I don't have a problem with that. What I do have a problem with is when you are hiding something from me. You chill, I like yo style, yo pussy good and you a shoota like me, but I don't do fucking secrets," I explained to her.

Asia came close to me, wrapping her arm around my neck. "So, you like me for real?"

I turned my head away from her. "Man, stop playing. I have no patience. I will kill a nigga on spot. You got to be on point fucking with me."

Peck to my neck, then peck to my lips.

Her lips were soft and juicy. I accepted her kiss, allowing her to suck on my lips. I took a hand full of her hair into my hand, gripping it, pulling her head slightly to the side. I dug my teeth into her neck, creating an impression. Her loud moans bounced off the walls. She went to pull off my shirt, "Nah mama not here. This is my bro office, but I got you. Hold that thought," I told her.

"Ok."

We headed back onto the main floor where everyone was. I spotted Harvey and Zu in the corner doing God knows what. Simone and the girl that Diamond was with were giving each other a stare down that didn't sit right with me. If it was easy for Asia to hide what she did, then it meant her friend could have been up to shady business as well. *Was Preach right?*

Diamond stood, coming over to me. "Where he at?"

"He should be here soon."

While we waited around for Chevy, my eyes stayed locked in on the two girls. Something wasn't right, and it was tugging at a nigga's gut. Shit was about to get spooky, and fast.

ZU

Harvey knew about the surprise we wanted to do for Chevy at Diamond's spot, and although she was against it, she came. She and I sat in the corner drinking and chilling for a bit. I admired shorty. She wasn't too different from the girls I dealt with in the past, but she had this energy that seem to match mine and it's what really drew me in. My only fear was if she got too attached and I fucked up what that would look like on the other end. She came from the same world as Chevy and the biggest thing with that was attachment issues. With him, he didn't want it, but with Harvey, it was like she needed it. Was I able to fill that missing void for her? This thing between us was fun. I wanted it to stay that way. However, Harvey she was looking for love, and I know it.

She rocked her body in the seat to the music. The short skirt she wore was turning a nigga on and I couldn't promise I could keep my hands to myself. I snatched by her waist, pulling her closer to me. "Why yo ass all the way over there?"

Harvey smiled, it was something about her smile that made all this feel like a schoolboy crush, and I have never felt that way. "I'm coolin'," she said to me.

My hands slid up her leg, but she slapped it away, "Man don't do that shit. This my pussy I can do what I want."

"Zu, this is my pussy and I decide when you can and cannot touch me."

I smacked my lips, then grabbed her face, squeezing her cheeks together. "Gimme a kiss."

Harvey slid her tongue across my lips, and I caught it. I like how she was just as nasty as me. She straddled my lap, bouncing her ass up and down. I gripped her ass cheek tight when someone came over with a camera. "Smile!"

Harvey and I threw up the middle finger at the say time and posed. She was like a calmer version of me, and I was finding myself becoming obsessed. It felt different when you had someone who was all about you. I was enjoying this ride, and I didn't want it to end. I wanted it to stay like this, nothing too heavy.

Hands back to her thighs. This time, she didn't stop me. My hand eased up her leg slowly until I reached her pussy. *Circle, Circle* around her clit.

"This shit wet as hell," I said, biting on my lip.

She winked. I removed my fingers, bringing it to my lips, sticking my finger in my mouth. If it wasn't for us waiting on

Chevy's ass, Harvey and I would be out of this bitch. She got up from my lap, stood, grabbing the bottle taking the liquor to the back of her throat. She looked so good standing there rocking her hips in that little ass skirt and my jacket. Orange went well with her complexion.

I spotted a few more people come into the building, then I heard them calling out animal noises. I knew Chevy had arrived. *"We don't fuck with you; we only fuck with da Zoo!"*

I stood walking over, but Harvey stopped me. She dug in her purse, "Here clean your hand nigga," she laughed.

Shit, I forgot all about it. I was more concern about him accepting this surprise. I knew I had fucked up and he and I hadn't talked since he walked out on us. I couldn't lose my friendship with my brother. It was bigger than the group. I hadn't even told Harvey I fucked up. I had a lot on the line and a lot to fix. The other guys dapped him up and were talking to him when I came up. Chevy looked at me but said nothing. "Chevy my nigga," I started.

He turned to me raising his chin, "Save it Zu, I'm here let's have a good time. Since you guys decided to do something for me, I'm going to enjoy it. Other than that, let's keep it short."

Chevy walked off to talk to some other people. I never thought I would see the day when Chevy and I wouldn't be talking to each other, let alone stop being friends.

HARVEY

I watched as Zu and Chevy interacted, but it was little to none. Something wasn't right. I waited for them to part ways before going over to Chev. When Zu came up to me, he wasn't the man who had just walked away from me only a few minutes ago. He stood there with sadness in his eyes. "What's wrong?"

Zu said nothing. Instead, he planted a kiss to my lips then went to sit down. I look back at him, then back at Chev, who was talking to people. I marched over to Foe because somebody needed to tell me something. The girl he was with had her arms wrapped around his neck, hugging the nigga so tight I thought she was choking his ass. I tapped his shoulder, making him turn toward me. "Waddup Harvey?"

She turned her face up at me like I was interrupting something important. "Can I talk to you for a second, please?"

He pulled away from her, walking me to a corner. Foe eyes landed on mine. He said nothing yet, he just stared at me and for a minute I thought I saw something in his eyes. Foe reminded me so much of Chev, only difference is I didn't see him as a brother, but a good friend. I cleared my throat before speaking. "Zu and Chev. What's going on with them?"

Foe glanced at them both. "It's not my business to tell. You know I don't do that," he said, pinching his lips together.

I tossed my hands on my hips, shifting my body to one side. "Nigga!"

He threw his hands up, "You said you been knowing Chev since you two were kids, right? Then it should be nothing for you to find out. Other than that, you straight?"

It was him caring enough to make sure I was Ok. Even the times he had taken me home, he always made sure I was straight. Just like Chev. I nodded my head, letting him know I was good. Foe winked, then walked off back to the girl who was impatiently waiting on him. I focus my attention back on Chev as I walked to over to talk to him. I tapped his shoulder. When he saw me, he flicked Zu's biker jacket. "I see you."

I embraced him in a hug. "How are you feeling?" I whispered in his ear.

"Straight, you good?"

"Always."

I titled my head so I could look in his eyes, "What's up with you and Zu?"

He ran his hand over his head. He always did that when he didn't want to talk about something. "Shit we straight," he mumbled.

"June!"

There was that look. "Stop calling me that shit. I let it slide in the hospital but not here. We good, nigga, just be making bad choices, ones that cost us money. That doesn't have anything to do with you, though. I told them I was leaving the crew."

My eyes grew. Now it was making sense why they were throwing this party. "You sure that's what you want to do?"

"I have no choice."

I didn't like how he was talking. Before I could get another word out, I heard a familiar voice. "Chevy!" Lola squealed.

She walked up to him, wrapping her arm around his neck, and the nigga accepted it. My head flew back.

"Hey Harve!"

"Hey Lo," I said dryly. "Who invited you?"

"Chevy did."

My eyes landed on him. "You said I need to find a woman, right?"

I did, but not her ass. Lola wasn't the one for Chevy. If he really got to know her, the shit wasn't going to last long at all. I grabbed him by his arm, pulling him away from her.

"She's not it."

"I said the same about Zu, but you chose otherwise."

The nigga always knew how to throw some shit back in your face. My lips tightly gripped each other. "You right."

"You decided if you were rolling with me? I'll be done with the caprice in no time."

I didn't even think about it since him telling me. Me and Zu had something going on and I wasn't ready to jump ship yet. Hell, Chevy found his mother. As for me, I didn't bother searching for my parents. With each passing year, I became more convinced that it wasn't worth my time and energy to find them. If they genuinely cared about me, they wouldn't have willingly given me up.

One minute was too long for him. With a single clap, he brought me back from my daydream. "I see you haven't. Well, you know my car door is always open to you."

Lola had now found her way back to us. She looked at Chevy and whispered something in his ear. He gave her a serious look. "The type of dick I serve is life changing. So, be careful what you ask for."

I could tell Lola was embarrassed, but that was one thing she needed to accept with him. The nigga was super direct. I left them standing there, walking to the bar.

"Can I get a shot please?"

While I waited for them to pour my drink, I glanced around, watching everyone have a good time. Each nigga with a female and Zu in the corner looking like a lost puppy. A familiar face entered the building, with three men behind her. She smiled brightly as she shook her hips to the beat. It was

Triece. That's what Chevy said her name was. I rolled my eyes because who invited her? I could tell she was looking for Zu. Just like I thought. As soon as she saw him, she trotted her ass right up to him.

It only pissed me off because he was talking to her. What was it they needed to talk about? The bartender tapped my shoulder, handing me my drink, and I took it back so fast. I slammed the glass down on the counter, getting ready to head that way when I felt a pair of hands to my arm.

"Don't do it," Foe said to me.

I glanced around for his goddamn magnet. "She went to the bathroom," he paused, then pointed to Triece. "Her brothers work for us, so she was bound to be around. Just chill," he said to me.

I squinted my eyes. "Why do you care about how I feel?"

"A friend of Chevy is a friend of mine. So, I'm begging you Harvey don't make me have to pull my gun out."

Foe walked off. I gave Zu another minute to get her out of his fucking face before I began fucking some shit up. That's when the DJ played my song, and I was about to make this nigga pay. I moved my way to the dance floor and began rocking my hips to the beat. *Bend forward, twerk, twerk, twerk.* Some random drunk guy came up behind me and grabbed my waist. *Leg lift, shake, leg lift shake.* At this point, I had forgotten all about Zu as I was feeling the music.

146

I could hear some of the crowd hyping me up and it only fueled me to dance more. I felt the guy's hand rubbing on my thighs, but I moved his hand only for him to put it back. "I'm about to peel yo shit back if you don't get yo fuckin hands off her," I heard Zu's voice.

I turned, and he had his gun to the side of the man's head. "Harvey unless you want me to open his head like a can of tomato soup you better get yo ass over there and sit down," he gritted.

"Zu, go talk to yo ex and leave me the fuck alone!" I hissed.

Bloaw! Bloaw!

Zu shot him in both his feet, "Shuck and jive now nigga!"

He grabbed me by shirt bringing me close to him. Chevy hand came between us, "We ain't doing that shit my nigga."

"Chev I'm good," I told him.

Zu picked me up and threw me over his shoulders, walking away from the dance floor.

"Man clean this shit up!" Chevy yelled.

Before Zu and I could get out the door, two girls started fighting. It was the girls who came with Zu's friends.

What the fuck was going on?

DIAMOND

Chilling with Mo was cool. It had been a minute since I've seen her since what went down. I wanted to wait a while after cutting her off. She was calling nonstop as I expected, but the showing up at the crib was wild. She'd actually showed up on the perfect day since we were having this little shindig for Chevy. The expectations of this party were for Zu to convince this nigga not to leave and to fix what he fucked up.

Shit was cool until Preach and Foe showed up. The girl Preach was with and Mo was being funny to each other the entire time. Mo, still being on my radar, I'd been watching her interaction with everyone the entire time. I was waiting on some shit to pop off and sure enough; it did. Between what happened at the bar and her fighting, Preach's date was putting her higher on the list.

They started whispering back and forth and at first, I was going to say something, but Foe came up to me and told he didn't trust either of them. So, I sat back and watched. The whispers became louder. From bitch this to hoe that. That's when they started fighting. I mean legit throwing hands straight hood shit. I picked up Mo, dragging her ass to the back. While Preach took his shorty out of the building.

When we got to the back office, Mo's panting was loud. Her hair was all over the place and her brown skin was now a reddish-brown color. Seeing her this angry was a turn on. Baby was mad as hell. *Fingers to her chin.* "Mo' what was that about?"

She huffed and puffed as she paced the floor. "I-I—"

I took her by her hand, bringing her toward me. With Mo, you had to be gentle. Me yelling at her wasn't going to get it. *Fingers to her chin.* I lifted it slightly so she could look at me. "Why were you fighting?"

"She just said some smart shit to me, and I couldn't take it."

I squinted my eyes. "You sure? Because if that's my nigga's girl she's going to be around and if y'all can't get along then you got to go, and I would hate to give up some good pussy over some dumb shit. So, I'm going to ask again. Why were you fighting?"

Mo's eyes bored into mine. I knew something was up, but I wanted her to tell me before I found out otherwise. She still said nothing. Tears welled up in her eyes. I held up my finger, walking back, locking the door. "Diamond what are you doing?"

"Shh," I said, placing my finger to my lips. "Sit in the chair Mo," I instructed her.

She was hesitant. "But I—"

I dropped my head, "Sit in the fucking chair Mo!"

This time she backed up, sitting in the chair. They way she looked at me as if she was trying to figure me out. She was trying her hardest to speak with her eyes, but I wasn't here for it.

I pointed. "Panties off. I'm only asking once."

She fumbled a little, but gradually pulled them off. I took my two fingers, opening them in a V shape, giving her the signal to spread her legs. "Yup just like that."

Mo sat there with her legs wide and her pretty brown pussy open, staring back at me. I could see she was nervous, but I didn't care. I stepped a closer. "Mo, I like you. I do, but it's something about you that has a nigga skeptical. I'm going to fuck you, not because you asked or because you out there fighting. I'm going to do it, one because I want to and two to give you something to hold you off til the next nigga bag yo ass because something is telling me you hiding shit."

She went to speak, and I held my hand up. "No, you don't get to speak because I asked you and you said nothing. One thing to learn about Zoo we don't lie, and we don't hide. So let me enjoy this moment. If you're true to your word, then you have nothing to worry about."

I got down on my knees, gripping her thighs, pulling her ass to the edge of the chair. I ran my tongue over the top of her pussy, then up and down her slit. "Sssss," she hissed. Mo's pussy was refreshing as I lapped around her clit a few times. Her body shuttered. "Mm, wait. Ah!" she cried.

"There is no wait Mo, this is what you wanted right?"

Face back down to her pussy. I circled and sucked on her so good I could feel her clit thump in my mouth. She moved her hips, thrusting in my face as her hands tugged on to my two braids, pulling me forward. Her breathing picked up. "I'm -I'm."

Her legs shook, body bucked, and she screamed so loud, I knew everyone on the other side of this door heard her. She just had an orgasm that snatched her soul. I lifted my head to see her eyes closed. She enjoyed it very much so. "You look sexy as fuck when you cum for me, let's do it again," I whispered.

Helping her up, I then bent her over my desk. I pulled her dress above her waist while pushing her body flat on the desk and entered her slowly. Mo's pussy was so wet I went into autopilot. "Damn girl. I hope you ain't no snake cause I don't want to give this up!" I grunted.

"Then do-don't," she stuttered.

Smack!

I started rolling my hips, trying my best to get further inside her. I wanted to be in her so deep that my dick would rearrange her insides. The sounds of her queefing filled the room. Two hands to her waist, as my head dropped forward. Shit felt so good. *"Bust that pussy open for a real one,"* I sang.

I bit into my lip. "Damn Mo this shit fire as fuck!" I growled.

I watched every time my dick played hide and seek inside her. "I'm sorry Diamond," she moaned.

She tried to reach to grab my hand, but I slapped them away. "Nah baby let me finish. I know you fucked up. It's too damn bad."

I began pounding harder. "Shit!"

Bam! Bam! Bam!

"Give me a minute!" I shouted.

Bam! Bam!

"Nigga she a snake!" I heard Preach voice.

I wanted to stop right then, but from the way her pussy muscles gripped me, I couldn't. Mo started throwing her ass back so good I had to squat a little to get in motion. I knew she was trying her best to fuck me out of my decision and although the feeling was casting a spell on me. I knew I had to end it.

"Mm baby, don't stop," she whimpered.

My arms crossed over her ass, "Goddamn Mo. I'm cumin'!" I yelled, picking up speed.

As soon as I felt the nut tickling the head of my dick, I pulled out. "Ah, shit!" I released myself.

I entered the adjoined bathroom cleaning myself up, leaving her ass bent over the desk. I came out to her standing there looking guilty. I headed for the door, but she ran in front of it with her arms stretched wide. "Diamond let me explain."

I smiled, stroking her pretty face. I got as close as I could to her lips. "We done Mo."

I moved her out of the way, opening the door. When she realized it was real, she straightened her dress and took the walk of shame out of the office, down the hall, and out of the building.

Now it was time to find out how dirty she really was. It was a sad day because I really liked Monette. I'd been praying the entire time she was one of the good ones, but she was trifling like the rest of the hoes.

So, it was now back to Zoo over everything.

Chapter Eight

ZU
Zoo 101

Everyone left the lounge but us. We all stood around, looking at each other. Chevy's tight face said he was ready to fuck some shit up. He sat in the chair with his elbows to his knees. "Talk to me," he said calmly.

Preach began explaining. "I knew something was up when Simone came into the church that day. Foe and I were being followed, but we handled it."

"Ok," Chevy said.

I jumped in, "Fuck all that get to the point."

They all looked at me. I shrugged. I was ready to get to the action. Preach kept going. "I started fucking with Simone because I had a funny feeling about her. I was trying to see what she knew and who she knew. I had got word she was with Nash's people, but I wasn't sure. But when her and Diamond's shorty got into it that's when it came out. What's her name, Monette? Well, she is Nash's cousin, and she was supposed to fuck with you, Chevy, but ended up fucking with Diamond. They wanted to take us out, guns and all. Nash is Clarence's people."

I could see Diamond's light skin ass turning red. *"Fuck!"* he shouted.

I knew he was mad he ended up fucking with an op. This was the one thing Chevy always talked about, us slipping up over some pussy. People knew about Zoo, and we had run shit, got away with shit for the longest. Who knew killing Clarence's bitch ass would lead to this? Chevy place prayer hands to his lips. He closed his eyes for a mere second, then looked at all four of us.

He began pointing, "This shit is not what were supposed to be about. How did we let *bitches* come in and stir the fucking pot? Huh?" He started as he got up from the chair. "Diamond, you're smarter than that so what's up talk to me? Is the pussy that good?"

Diamond stood there. "I had a feeling but wasn't sure."

Chevy nodded. "You had a feeling, so why you didn't go with it?"

He said nothing. Chevy then turned to Preach, "Of all people the pickiest nigga of the bunch. You should've handled it immediately. Preach the prayer, the nigga that's always preaching about good and evil and the demon was staring you in the face how did you not see that? So we fucking demons now?"

I knew Chevy was conjuring up some evil shit to do. When a nigga stepped on his toes, it was war and I was ready. I've always hated Nash since back in the day. However, Nash's hate for Chevy was more like an obsession. He hated Chevy, had always seemed to come out on top in everything he did. How most looked up to him instead of down on him. The nigga thought because he was a loner, didn't have a family that he would fail. Chevy had legal businesses, investments and other things he dabbled in. He was really sitting on top.

Then the Zoo Boyz emerged, and it was really the icing on the cake. We were crushing the illegal streets races and making crazy bread with the gun business. It took years for Chevy to agree to race the Knights, and he only did it because he knew how to get under Nash's skin.

That's when something came to mind, "Yo Chevy, remember you told me Triece is fucking that nigga?"

"Triece smashing Nash big ass?" Foe blurted out.

Chevy and I both shot him a look. I continued. "She knows a lot about us. Who goes to say she ain't helping him also," I added.

Chevy nodded. "I want them nigga's heads. When I finish with them, if any are left standing, I want them to realize how savage we are. I will handle Triece's brothers."

Foe stepped up. "I will find out where them niggas hang out and we can set some shit up."

Chevy went to leave, then stopped and turned to us. "This is my last time protecting Zoo. Y'all niggas need to get your shit in order."

With that, he left. "*Fuck!*" Diamond screamed.

He must have liked this girl a lot. I'd never seen the nigga so mad before. For the first time, I wasn't in the spotlight. However, I knew I had to fix this. I left, headed to Triece's. Nigga was doing a hundred trying to get to her. I wanted to talk her out of whatever it was she was thinking. When she came up to me, she was popping a lot of shit. I was used to it, though. They were mostly empty threats, but with her knowing me and Harvey were chilling, she was capable of any fucking thing. I also wanted to know what she was feeding Nash.

It took me all of fifteen minutes to get to her crib. When I pulled up, one of her brothers had come outside standing on the porch. When he saw me, he ran back in the house, and I was on his ass. By the time I got in, he had run through the back door, and I knew some shit was up. I began searching the house, but no one else was in there. I left, sending Triece a text because she and I needed to talk.

While I waited to hear from her, I went to pay Harvey a visit because the stunt she pulled tonight; her showing off, letting niggas rub all on her. I wasn't having it. Clearly, she didn't understand how I operated. It was time to teach her Zoo 101. Once I arrived, I rushed to her door banging on that muthfucka. When she opened the door, she stood there, just staring.

"Clothes the fuck off!" I snapped.

She rolled her eyes. "Zu please!"

"Exactly what your ass about to be saying. I said clothes off!"

I pushed my way in the house, closing the door behind me. "Zu you thinking fucking is going to change me begin mad at you it's not. So no, I won't take my clothes off." She folded her arms over her chest.

I leaned against the wall, "Harvey do it look like I'm playing? Take. That. Shit. Off. Now!"

She smacked her lips, but she came out of every piece of clothing she had on. Her standing there naked looked like chocolate perfection. I came off the wall, approaching her. My tall frame towered over her. "Turn around and bend over."

Harvey laughed. "What?"

I put my hands to her cheeks, squeezing them together. I place my lips on hers, "I said turn around and bend the fuck over," I growled.

Her eyes softened. I released her and she turned, bending over. However, the way she did it was purely seductive. I came out of my clothes. I grabbed my dick, tapping her ass with it. I could hear a soft moan escape her. "It's time to teach you that the only nigga who touches you like that is me. Can't no nigga do to you what I do."

I slid my dick up and down her pussy lips until I entered her. Harvey gasp loudly. "Inch by inch," I mumbled.

I took both her arms, bringing them back. As I leaned forward, my tongue glided up and down her back. That's when I lifted her from the floor and begin using her ass like a slinky.

"Zu!" she whined.

Her feet clung on to my waist.

Up, then down.

"This pussy belongs to Zu," I growled.

Harvey moans sounded like cries turning me on and up more.

Up, then down.

"Zu please!"

Up, then down.

"No ain't no Zu please. Take this dick!"

Up, then down.

"You wanted to be touched right, so take all of it baby."

I shuffled my feet to get better leverage, kicking my pants out of the way, sending my phone forward. I saw the phone light up but couldn't really see the screen.

Up, then down.

Harvey tussled out of my grasp, making me put her down. "Fuck is you doing man?"

"Zu get out!" she screamed. "The bitch is texting you!"

Harvey just needed to let me explain because she was overreacting. "Man chill it's not even like that," I told her.

She picked my shit up, throwing it out of her house. "You got two seconds to get the fuck out or it's going to get real zoo like in this bitch!"

I put my hand over my dick walking out of her crib. I couldn't even turn to say anything before she slammed the door in my fucking face. I couldn't lie. I was mad as hell.

For the first time, a nigga did nothing.

MONETTE

After calling an Uber to get me home, all I wanted to do was crawl in my bed and cry myself to sleep. I could imagine all the things being said about me once I left. This is not how I wanted things to play out. Simone, threating to say something, pissed me off. We went from light whispers to a full-blown fight. I was going to tell Diamond I just wanted to be in the right atmosphere. When I told him, I wanted him to be so into me that if anything were to happen to me, he would protect me. I'd started falling for Diamond after the first night of being together. I liked him more than I should have. What I thought would be something simple as getting to know him for information turned into something completely unexpected. Diamond was definitely a rare breed from the way he acted to how he talked to me, so calm, so cool, but underneath all that, a man who was a protector, by any means. The man fucked my brains out before cutting me off.

I hated I let my cousin talk me into this. I should have just said no. He took my desperate need for help to the next level.

Nash was crazy. He was capable of anything. He hated to lose and in this situation; he was losing.

I had only been home for about ten minutes before someone was banging on my door. I thought about not answering it, but if it was Diamond, I wanted a chance to explain. I wanted him to look in my eyes to see how sorry I was. I rushed over to the door, swinging it open. Nash and two of his guys rushed inside with big ass bags in their hands. "I need to hide this here."

I rushed behind Nash, who was moving through my place, opening different doors.

"No, take that shit out of here. I don't want nothing to do with it."

He stacked the bag in a hall closet. He turned to me, looking scared as hell.

"Get that shit out of here!" I screamed.

"Monette please!" he roared. "Just for tonight I will get it in the morning, I just need it to stay here for the night."

Nash was sweating profusely, breathing heavy. He looked like he had gotten into a fight, and it scared me. "What did you do?"

Nash said nothing as he and his friends left my place, slamming the door behind them. *Goddamnit!* I waited a few minutes as I stared at the closet. Curiosity was eating me alive. I walked over to the closet where they had placed the bags. I open the door and was about to peek into the bag when there was another bang on my door. I didn't know what type of games Nash was playing, but I was done with the bullshit. I rushed over to the front door, swinging it open ready to cuss his ass out, "Nash please!"

"So, you do know the nigga?" Diamond gritted.

My eyes widen. "Diamond what are you doing here?"

He stepped toward me, and I stepped back, "I came because I wanted you to look me in my face and tell me all the shit I heard was a fucking lie. That I didn't serve good dick to an op!" he barked.

I was speechless. I didn't know what to say. "You gone stand there or say something? Huh? Cause right now I can ring your fucking neck. My nigga, my big brother looking at me sideways because I trusted you and yo ass ain't nothing but a fraud. Starting with my grandma. I should have left yo ass alone then."

"Diamond I was going to tell—"

The sound of something falling caught both of our attention. I looked back, and the bags had fell out the closet. A bunch of fucking guns. This could not be happening to me. I had the worst luck with this entire situation.

"The fuck is that!" Diamond yelled, pushing past me.

"I-I don't know," I mumbled.

He approached the guns, picking them up and looking at them. "Oh, yo ass shady for real. He tossed them back in the bag, taking them and heading for the door.

"I swear I didn't know those were in there."

"Yeah, and I swear I'm done with yo ass. Mo, lose my fucking number!" He said as he walked right out the door.

Nash didn't have to do anything at this point because he had already fucked up my life. Diamond and I brief time together felt like heaven and I allowed my cousin to drag me straight to hell. There was nothing I could say. As I was going to do before, I went into my room to cry myself to sleep.

Chapter Nine

HARVEY
Pull up Game

Tonight, I was going out. One of my clients invited me to her birthday party at the local strip club. I'd tried chilling with Chevy, but Lola had been occupying his time. Zu had called me a few times, but I hit the ignored button on him. I really thought Zu was for me, but he just proved Chevy right and I hated to admit it. Since he couldn't leave Triece alone, I was leaving his ass alone.

I dressed a little risky tonight. I wore an all-black knitted dress with black high-waisted panties and black bra. A pair of clear heels and a cute black clutch bag. I spotted a few of the Knights' bikes outside, so I knew there were many people inside. Once I was in the club, all I saw was money being tossed in the air, coming down like confetti. There were so many people it was barely space to walk. I traveled through the club to find my girl section until I felt someone's hand grab

165

my wrist. I glanced down to see a fine ass nigga looking up at me. He pulled me down toward him. "You look good as hell," he somewhat yelled in my ear.

I smiled, nodding my head. I tried lifting to walk away, and he pulled me down again, trying to talk to me. "Where you going? You don't fuck with the Knights or what?"

I licked my lips, smiling at him. I placed my lips to his ear. "I only fuck with da Zoo!" I howled.

I started laughing when he pushed me away. There was no way, no matter how fine, I would talk to a crew Chevy didn't get along with. I began making my way through club until I spotted my girl. They had the section lit. Bottles on bottles and stacks of money to throw on the girls. Things were cool for a minute until I spotted Foe, then Zu, and one after the next, with Chevy coming in last. The way they stayed pulling up on people was crazy. The looks on their faces said they were up to no good and something in my stomach turned.

The DJ had announced the next dancer. "Coming to the stage the only one who can make shit hot up in here. They call her Spicy."

When I glanced at the stage, it was the girl that was hugged up with Foe. *What the fuck is going on?* The song she was dancing to spoke volumes. These niggas were up to something. I looked back over at them as they strolled through the club like they owned it. Foe glanced at the stage, looking at her, shaking his head. He placed his finger to his lips while pulling a mask down over his face. The shit was like slow motion as he pulled a gun from behind him. The black light flashed over them, creating a sense of get the fuck up and run. Chevy ran up, jumping on stage. The black light illuminated his dark skin beautifully. The dark demon emerged from him as his chest heaved in and out. He looked like he was ready to dominate. His eyes bounced on his crew as he nodded. Chevy was giving pure muhfuckin' king. He held a choppa in his hand that rested on his side. I only knew what it was because it was the first gun he taught me to shoot. Shit was about to go down, and fast.

I turned to my girl, trying to snatch her down. "Yo, get the fuck down!" I screamed.

Rat tat tat tat tat! Rat tat tat tat tat!

He shot in the air. The DJ cut the music, taking off along with the crowd of people who started hauling ass everywhere. I dropped to my knees, crawling, glancing between the tables. They began fighting the Knights. You could hear the grunting and bullets whistling everywhere. My friend stood and started running. What I didn't want was for her to get shot, so I stood running behind her to pull her down. "Harvey!" I heard someone scream my name.

I turned to look and the same nigga I shitted on had a gun aimed at me.

Zu crept up behind him, placing the barrel to the back of his head. "Close yo eyes, baby," I heard him say.

I didn't have time before he pulled the trigger.

Bloaw!

The guy's head damn near exploded. I froze. I couldn't move. Zu came over to me, yanking my arm. "Get the fuck out of here. What you got on? Tryna catch a nigga. Go home!"

My feet just wouldn't move. The gun shots subsided and the smoke from all the shooting cleared. I spotted two dead bodies and most of the Knights' crew crawling on the ground. Chevy walked over to the biggest dude. He must have been the leader because he stood there, chin up, ready to take an L. Chevy aimed the choppa at his face, gritting his teeth. "Nash, nigga you caused all this shit. You got dead niggas on your hands." Chevy started. "You tried to sabotage the race, you tried to set us up and you stole from me, can't nothing save you *my nigga!*" he yelled so loud the shit snapped me out of the trance I was in.

The big guy started laughing because he knew his demise. He flicked his nose. "You killed my cousin!" he screamed back. "What was I supposed to do? Let you slide?"

"Nah nigga you were supposed to step to me!"

The guy cocked his gun back he had in his hand.

Chevy showed no fear as he stepped closer to him. He brought the choppa down to the man's stomach, pressing the barrel in his big belly. "You want to get skinny nigga! This lead will go in you so fast put yo fat ass on a permanent weight loss plan!" Chevy snapped.

I didn't want to see him do it. I couldn't. "Chev no!" I yelled.

Zu turned to me. "Don't do that. Let him handle this shit. You know nothing about this. You shouldn't even be here," Zu said to me.

I cut my eyes at him because I didn't want him talking to me. I knew Chevy much better than he did. I knew once you took Chevy there; it was hard for him to come back. He had changed so much over the years. This would set him back, and I just couldn't let him do it. "Chev please don't. Handle this a different way," I begged.

Chevy looked at me, and I shook my head. *No,* I mouthed. Chevy lowered his gun. "Better thank the lady," he said as he walked off.

The owner rushed out screaming. Chevy looked at Preach, nodding his head. He tossed the old man a bag as they all followed behind him, leaving. Zu didn't move. Instead, he stood there staring at me, "Man if you don't get yo ass out of here!"

Zu's patience was gone. He picked me up, throwing me over his shoulders. "Zu put me down!"

"Fuck that! Harvey, you sold your soul to Zu ain't no backing out."

When we got outside, he put me down, following me all the way to my car, "Go to my house."

"No!" I hissed, getting into my car.

Zu swung the door open. "I see you in twenty minutes. Harvey don't make me come looking for you. You see the type of damage we do. If you don't want somebody else's brains marinating in the concrete I suggest you be there," he said, closing the door.

He jogged back over to his bike. In unison, they all sped off together. I wanted to go home, but I didn't have time to play with Zu, so I headed to his house.

FOE

Asia looked out by letting me know the Knights were going to be at the club. Seeing her on stage, I thought I would be mad that she was shaking her ass for other niggas. However, I respected the hustle. I knew what it was like trying to get it by any means. If she was loyal to the soil, all was good. In that moment I had to pull my feelings out of it because it was about Zoo and not her.

She was to meet me at my crib and bring Simone with her. Tonight, little did they know we were going to clear some shit up. After leaving the club, we all split. We needed to let things cool down for a while after the stunt we just pulled. Not to mention Zoo day was approaching. We needed to have clear heads in case the Knights tried to retaliate. Nash, he knew what it was, but knowing that nigga, he was going to try some shit.

Preach and I chilled until I got the text that they were outside. I got up from the couch to open the door. They both stood there looking simple as hell. Before I could let them in, I felt Preach push past me, snatching Simone in the crib. "Damn Preach you're hurting me," Simone whined.

"I don't give a fuck!" he shouted.

They both stood in the middle of the living room floor. "Simone, you tried me. You played in my face and because of you we had to make example out of niggas!"

Simone couldn't say shit as he kept going. "I'm about to lose my mind and my religion fucking with you." He pointed at her. "The night you were fighting I let you slide because you were super emotional and shit, but I knew since the day you walked in the church you were shady. I figured hell, let me give her some dick and maybe she would say something, yo ass said nothing!"

"Yo nigga chill on my girl, damn!" Asia shouted.

I placed my hand to her stomach, "Nah we ain't doing that mama."

Asia looked at me, rolling her eyes. "That's my best friend and what he's not about to do is shit on her like that."

"And that nigga is my best friend and what you not about to do, is come in here tryna run some shit. See, you said that's yo best friend so that means the right hand knows what the left hand is doing," I paused. Now in her face. "If that is correct then you knew all along, she was playing us which means you're just as fucked up!"

Asia's mouth was open, but she didn't say nothing. I watched her eyes and just as I figured, guilty. "Shits crazy man because I liked you. I thought you were one of the real ones." She reached out to me, but I pulled away.

"Foe I am, I-I—"

"Save it mama. I don't want to hear it."

The sound of Simone crying made me turn around. "Preach I told you everything because I didn't want to be a part of it anymore. Nash, he—"

"Just tell him Simone," Asia whispered.

Preach stepped to Simone, lifting her chin, "Tell me."

"He has a tape of me. I got drunk at one of their parties and things happened."

Preach face changed. The nigga went from frustrated to angry. The thing about Preach. He will forgive her because he had that type of heart, but he may never give Simone another chance. He was still a protector, though, and that alone was going to save her. It was something Chevy taught all of us.

I knew he had some crazy shit going through his head. All the holy shit was about to go right out the window. "They raped you?" he asked her.

Simone looked down, then back up at him. "I wouldn't say rape, but I was so drunk I didn't know—"

"They did!" Asia shouted.

Just what Zoo needed to be involved in another bloodbath. I knew what Preach was thinking. "Shit we got most of them," I told him.

"But not Nash's fat ass! Let's go!" he shouted.

I ran my hand through my dreads. "Fuck!"

The ideal thing to do would have been to call Chevy, but this was about to get nasty and I didn't want my nigga involved. All four of us hopped in his car. Preach hauled ass through the streets. Simone was directing him to Nash's crib. Asia placed her hand on my leg. "Asia get yo crumb snatchers off me. Just because this nigga wants to be superman don't mean you and I are cool."

Once you fucked me over, I wasn't looking back. Loyalty was a number one for me, and I knew I couldn't trust Asia. "You said you were mine," she whispered.

"Yeah, well, I lied like you."

When we pulled up to Nash's crib, Preach and I looked at each. "Y'all stay in the car," he told the girls.

We crept up to his raggedy ass crib. The way Nash lived; you would think the nigga was broke. He lived in a beat-up ass house, one that was probably handed down by family and he never took care of it. However, the nigga had a little bread he was sitting on. Preach wasted no time kicking the door in, sending the glass crashing down. "Damn for a skinny nigga you got ninja feet."

When we stepped inside, Nash's head shot up and Triece's head came up from his lap. "Bitch you sucking dick!" I shouted.

She immediately started going off. "Why the fuck y'all here. Y'all need to—"

Preach wasted no time drilling on Nash's head. "Fuck nigga you like raping women!" I'd never seen him go so hard. "I'll pray about it later, but you gone get this work," he gritted.

Triece's ass was screaming at the top of her lungs. I aimed my gun at her. "If you don't close that fucking fly trap, I'm going to put a bullet in you!"

Preach pounded on Nash's head so much the shit was bouncing back like basketball. I ran up to him, "Enough!" I shouted.

Preach chest heaved in and out. When he looked at me, his eyes flickered. "You like her don't you," I whispered.

He snatched the gun out of my hand, cocking it back. "Triece, I better see yo ass at church on Sunday. Get yo funky, nasty ass out of here," he told her.

She hurried running around the couch to get out of the door. "Nash, let's pray," Preach told him.

I closed the door because I knew Nash's time was about to be up. I grabbed the pillow sitting next to him, about to place it over his face. When Simone came running through the door, "Preach don't!" she screamed.

"Go get back in the car and stay there like I said!" he shouted at her.

She eased her way up to him. "Preach please. You've done enough and I appreciate you, I swear. What would your dad think if you killed someone," she told him.

It's too late for all that shit. Preach and his father's relationship was a tough one. He wanted his son out of the street and in the church. It was something Preach had straddle the fence about. Not that he didn't believe in God because he did, but he felt like he was serving two Gods. The in the church and the one in the streets. His father's acceptance meant a lot to him. He lowered the gun and glanced at Simone. She took him by his hand, pulling him outside.

I went to follow him until Nash started talking shit. "You Zoo niggas are dead!"

I closed the door, walking back over to him. "The difference between me and that nigga, I don't give a fuck."

I put the nigga in a chokehold and snapped his neck. Whether or not God forgives me, Nash was now one less problem we needed to worry about.

ZU

When I got home, Harvey was waiting on me. She had fallen asleep in her car. I stood there watching her sleep, thinking of what she had just experienced. I knew Chevy didn't involve her in that kind of thing. It was clear why he kept her distant from our world. However, now that she was fucking with me, it was bound to happen. I tapped on the window, waking her up. She unlocked the door and went to get out, but I picked her up, carrying her into my house. "Zu I can walk," she whispered.

"I know baby but your tired so I'm carrying you."

Once we were inside, I put her down. I wanted to show some type of compassion for what she was just exposed to.

"I know you're shaking up by what you saw."

Harvey's intense glare told me she was afraid. Seeing her look so fragile and so scared made me feel something. I pulled her in, hugging her tightly. I lead her up to my room. We stood in the dark, looking at each other. I realized the way I felt about her had changed. I could say that I cared for her a lot. I slid her dress off, then her bra, then her panties. I was unsure about being romantic or showing tenderness, but Harvey motivated me to give it my best shot. I removed my clothing and got into the bed. "Come here let me hold you."

Harvey climbed in, but instead of lying next to me, she climbed on top of me and that was even better. I've been with a lot of women, including Triece, but I've never felt like I do about her. I could have easily fucked her, but I didn't want to. I wanted to do what we were doing now. Holding each other. "I was just trying to protect you baby that's all."

"I know," she whispered.

"Since that day you and I smashed I have not slept with Triece, I swear," I told her.

I found myself explaining, which was some shit I've never done. She lifted her head to look at me. I needed her to understand I was trying.

"I promise. I did not. I like you. A nigga really fucks with you heavy. I'm not perfect but for you I'm trying."

Harvey's smile lit up the dark space. She kissed me. *Peck to the lips, another, then another.*

Simple kisses turned into a nasty tongue battle. She pulled her lips from me. "I want you to put your face in it." She smiled.

"On my face."

She looked at me in confusion. "Sit on my face," I repeated.

Harvey inched her way up toward my face. She looked down. "I don't want to smother you," she whispered.

I clung onto her thighs. "I want you to. Let my tongue make love to your pussy. You just enjoy it," I said as I lowered her down on my face.

I closed my eyes, imagining all the things Harvey and I had ahead. I parted her lips with my tongue and went to work. I licked and sucked on her like she was the last meal I'll ever taste. I wanted to consume her soul. Her body leaned forward, and her hips rocked.

"I swear this feels so good," she moaned.

Harvey moans started off low and sweet, then became boisterous. "Goddamn Zu!"

Her hand landed on top of my head as she began pulling at my dreads. "Ah!" she cried.

I flicked faster, sucked harder. I wanted to see her face as she reached ecstasy, so I lifted her, sending her backwards, lying her on her back, allowing her legs to rest over my shoulder. "I want to watch you cum, baby," I told her.

I removed my mouth, taking two fingers and placing them inside her. I watch every expression Harvey gave as my fingers played with her. "You look so good when you cum for me."

"I'm cumin Zu!" she screamed.

My fingers didn't stop until her body bucked as her last moan bounced off my bedroom walls. We didn't even bother to get out of the bed afterwards. Instead, she let me hold her until she fell asleep. I laid there thinking how happy I was that I met her. Honestly, I should thank Chevy because he brought her around.

Chapter Ten

MONETTE
Zoo Day

The sun peeked through my curtains, as I didn't realize I had fallen to sleep. I dragged myself out of bed and headed straight to shower. Once I was done, I wanted to go by Diamond's grandmother's house to apologize. She probably didn't know what was going on, but I felt bad and needed to take accountability for what I did. By the time I had gotten dressed, two hours had gone by. I must have been moving slowly, because it had never taken me this long to get ready.

I thought about calling Diamond or at least text him, letting him know I was going over that way so it wouldn't be any surprises. When I picked up my phone, noticing thirty missed calls and a bunch of text messages from my family. I opened my text messages and the first thing I saw made my stomach drop. Nash was dead. Nash was evil, but he was my family. The only person who could have done something like this was

Diamond. The last time I saw him, he was so mad it only made sense.

I snatched my purse and left the house. I sped down the highway to get downtown. I didn't know why there was a traffic backup. I picked up my phone to call Diamond, but it went straight to voicemail. He blocked me. *Fuck!* I maneuvered through the traffic until I found my exit. I pulled up to his condo in a matter of minutes. I stormed in the condominium's lobby, rushing to the elevator. When I finally reached his floor, I went to get off and a girl was coming in. She was pretty, pretty as hell. I knew she was there with Diamond, and it really pissed me off. He probably served her some of the same dick he gave me.

I couldn't believe him. He couldn't wait to cut me off so he could mess with the next bitch. Jealousy simmered in me so deep I had forgotten to get off the damn elevator. She glanced at me and smiled. *Ugh!* "Hi!" she squealed.

I quickly pulled the stop button, turning to her. She looked at me like I was weird, but I didn't care. I began pointing at her. "You think you're somebody because he fucked you? Huh?" I began rambling. "Don't fall for that shit. Yes, the dick is good. Real good, but just how he replaced me he will replace you. Matter of fact, that's my nigga and I'll be damn if I let a hollow head bitch like you come in and think you're about to swoop him from me."

She went to speak, but I stopped her. "I don't want to hear it. I get it you didn't know he had a girl, but he does. Diamond is mine!"

Her face balled up as she looked at me. "Who the fuck is Diamond? I was there to see Malik. You are aware there is more than one Condo on the top floor. Girl, you need help."

I shot her a quick smile. I felt so stupid. I hit the button, allowing the elevator to continue to go down. I scooted back to the corner, embarrassed as hell. I couldn't believe I was acting like this. When the elevator stopped, she went to get off but turned towards me. "If the dick makes you act like that, you don't need it," she said, getting off.

The doors closed, and I went back up. "Monette, get your shit together. You are tripping girl," I mumbled to myself.

Once I was back on his floor, I got off, rushing to his door. I knocked, but there was no answer. I knocked repeatedly, waiting for him. Someone came out of their condo across the way, looking at me. "He's gone."

"What?" I replied.

"You're knocking on Diamond's door. Are you looking for him?"

"Yes."

The gentleman smiled. "Diamond's my boy. It's Zoo day, his biker crews block party," he said.

I smiled nervously, "Oh right. Do you know where they're having it at?"

He glared at me, confused. Hell, I was confused. However, when he told me where it was, it all made sense. I left and head to where Diamond was. He had some explaining to do, and I wasn't stopping until I got answers.

DIAMOND

"Granny, you ready?" I asked.

Her ass was moving slower than a turtle. Typically, we would have Zoo day at a nearby park. Chevy opted for a block party theme this year. Instead of taking my grandma to a park, we organized Zoo day on her block. The event had a DJ, a stage for performers, various vendors, including food, barbers, hairstylists, after-school programs, and donation booths. Chevy covered the entire cost. There were other biker crews there to celebrate with us. The entire shit was a vibe.

My grandma had finally come out of her bedroom over to me. She looped her arm in mine as we stepped outside. Her eyes widen when she saw all the festivities on her block. The brown and orange colors stood out. "See, granny we ain't bad niggas. Bikers got a soul too," I laughed. *"Speak lord! Speak to me!"* I sang.

I knew my grandma loved to hear my voice. So, now and then I would throw something out there. I walked her outside, down the porch to a special spot we had for her. Once I made sure she was settled, I walked away for a few.

I spotted Zu and Harvey helping some kids. "Yo Zu where the fuck is Chevy?"

"The nigga ain't here yet?"

"Nah."

He looked at Harvey, who shrugged her shoulders. "I'll call him," she said as she pulled out her phone.

It was odd that he wasn't here. He was usually the main one walking around, making sure things were in order. Stuff like this meant a lot to him. He enjoyed giving back, especially to the kids in need. Harvey looked at us. "He didn't answer. Give him some time I'm sure he will be here soon."

He better had, or I was going to go look for him myself. I walked up the block to check things out. Preach and his father were at both handing out church pamphlets taking donations. While Foe was on the other side blowing up balloons. I wanted to keep my head on the swivel just in case the Knights came trying to fuck shit up.

I headed back toward my grandma when I spotted Mo talking to her. *Fuck is she here for?* My paced picked up as I made my way closer to them. She leaned over and was doing something. I snatched her arm back. "Get yo hands off my granny!" I spat.

"Chew! Stop!" my grandma shouted.

Mo peered at me. "Fuck is you mad for you the one that fucked up not me," I snapped.

I felt a slap to my leg. "Boy watch yo damn mouth in front of me. That's not how you talk to a lady," she started nagging.

I grabbed Mo by her arm, dragging her toward my grandma's house. "Fuck is you here for?"

She snatched her arm away from me. "Diamond why did you do it? Huh? You could have just walked away!" she yelled.

I didn't know what she was talking about. "What?"

She crossed her arms over her chest, "Stop playing dumb! You killed Nash!"

My head flew back. "I didn't touch his fat sloppy ass. I should have but I didn't!"

The last I saw Nash, we had left him standing there in the club unscathed. So, her talking about me killing him I didn't understand. Hell, he deserved what he got, not just for what he did to Zoo, but anyone else he'd fucked over.

I pinched the bridge of my nose. "Mo you sounding real crazy. Nobody touched that nigga. So, before you start making assumptions, please know what you're talking about."

"Diamond you were the only one mad storming out of my house like that. Now he's dead. No one else wanted to hurt him as bad as you did."

"Shittin' me. Your cousin was a fuck nigga. Maybe you don't know him like that, but we've been dealing with him for years. Why are you really here? Huh? I'm not fucking with you."

That cut her and cut her deep. I didn't know if she thought coming to me with this shit was going to make me beg her to be with me. I was done with Mo. Even if I thought about giving her another chance, a part of me wouldn't be able to trust her.

She reached out to me, grabbing my hand. "Diamond I'm sorry. Things weren't supposed to go like that. I like you a lot and—"

The sound of people screaming caught my attention. *"We only fuck with da Zoo!"*

I knew Chevy had arrived. I walk away from Mo, but she pulled me back. "Diamond were not done talking."

"Yes, we are Mo, we are."

I left her standing there while I went back over to my crew. Monette coming into my life was fun while it lasted. She reminded me how I needed to be more careful with women rather than being quick to fuck with them.

FOE

The day started off well. The city came out to celebrate with Zoo. We had the block packed. Preach and I decided not to tell Chevy about Nash. We let people believe what they wanted. I told him we should have gotten Triece's ass too, but the rule was never to touch women or children.

It took Chevy a minute to arrive, but when he did, you knew it because people gravitated toward him. When he pulled up, though, it wasn't on his bike. He pulled up in a clean ass orange Chevy caprice. The sun bounced off his chrome rims. The rattling sound coming from it hit so hard, letting me know he had a fire ass system in that bitch. We all walked over to him. He got out of the car talking to the kids that were admiring his ride. "Damn nigga this shit fly as hell!" I told him.

"I see you finished your project," Harvey jumped in.

I glanced at her because the way she said it had some attitude behind it. "Yeah, I had to pick it up today after they finished the inside but she ready to go," he replied.

"Go? Where the fuck you going?"

Chevy cut his eyes at me. "We'll talk about it later. Right now, let's enjoy today. Can we do that?"

Diamond had now walked up. "This bitch clean! Oowee, nigga got the orange and brown croc skin inside. I see you Chev!"

Something didn't make sense, and waiting for an answer would not work. As everyone walked ahead of us, I pulled him back. "Yo what the fuck is this shit? You leaving?"

Chevy turned to me. "Foe watch how you talk to me," he said as he flicked his nose. "I told y'all I was leaving Zoo. What I do with my time outside of y'all is my business. So again, we will talk about it later."

Chevy was leaving California. I knew him. He was up to something. I figure us riding together the other night would convince him to stay with the crew, but it seems like I was mistaken. He walked off and begin interacting with the kids and people. I went to go back to what I was doing, but felt a tap to my shoulder. I turned to see Asia standing there.

"You gone ignore me or we gone talk?" she said to me.

Walking away from her was my first thought, but I decided against it. "Ok, talk."

She stood there, fumbling with her hands. "Damn why you acting like that? I thought we had something."

I could see it was hard for her to even show a pinch of emotion. Nothing about Asia showed she was sorry. What she wanted was for me was to let shit roll off my shoulders and move on. It wasn't how I operated.

"We did have something mama. We made a connection I will admit that, but you can't even be real with me. You allowed yo friend to do some shady shit that could have not only cost me my life but my freedom."

"You cost yourself your own freedom. Nobody told y'all to go on a killing spree. Y'all could fought and left it at that."

I clapped my hands together. "And this is why I can't be with you. If you can't ride with me the way I need you to then there is no us. I did what the fuck I had to and it's clear you know nothing about it. Asia, dawg just go before you make me snap," I gritted.

I knew entertaining her was over before I lost my shit. I back pedal away from her slowly. "I know you killed Nash!" she yelled.

My feet couldn't move fast enough to get back to her. "Watch what the fuck you saying out here. I ain't do shit!"

I shook my head. "Yeah, you really ain't the shorty for me. Fuck you, Asia!"

I just walked away. Preach jog up to me. "Yo you aight? I just saw Simone and she was talking crazy."

I turned back to look at Asia, and she was gone. "Asia was too," I told him.

We both went back to what we were doing. From what Preach said to how Asia was acting, things didn't sit right with me, but for now I had to let it slide. They called all of us over for a group picture. We stood there posing for the camera when I spotted the police walking up to us. *I fucking knew it.*

"Zeus Jackson, Prentice Kingston, Diamond Blanco, Myles Thorton, and June Calloway?" the officer called out to all five of us.

Chevy stepped up to them. "What can we do you for?"

More police came up, arresting all of us. Harvey began screaming at them, but Chevy looked at her. "We good, chill," he said calmly.

Preach father walked alongside of him, praying. "The devil is a lie. My son did nothing. I rebuke you saint in the name of Jesus."

Preach dropped his head in shame. Diamond's grandma stood barely able to stand. "Chew!"

They walked us off to the police cars that were lined up waiting on us; I heard the office say Nash's name. Somebody snitched, and the only person who came to mind was Asia. *Fuckin' bitch!*

They tossed us in separate cars hauling our asses down to county. When we got there after processing us, we were all placed in cold stinky ass cell. We all knew not to say anything. Chevy sat there calm than a muhfucka, but I knew in the back of his mind he was ready to kill all of us. When they gave him phone time, he walked out and was gone for about ten minutes before he came back.

His eyes bounce on each one of us in disappointment. We sat around and waited until the officer came to the cell opening the gate. "Y'all are free to go," he said with an attitude.

I knew he had to make some calls to get us out. He paid our bail because he felt responsible for us. Chevy somehow making this shit go away. We owed him. We walk out of there, got our shit and left the building. A dark tinted black SUV was waiting for us when we stepped outside. As soon as we got in, Chevy snapped. "Who the fuck did it!" he screamed.

Nobody said anything. "Oh, so now you talkin' ass niggas ain't got shit to say! I knew he was dead last night. I got the call. I was prepared for today but clearly you niggas wasn't. I can't keep doing this shit. This is another reason I'm leaving Zoo!" He barked.

Diamond sat up. "It was probably Mo who snitched Nash is her cousin. She came up talking crazy today. I should have known."

"Or Simone. Hell, maybe Asia?" Preach jumped in.

Chevy nodded. "So again, bitches are the ones that shitted on us yet again!"

"Shit I was with Harvey all night. I ain't in this shit," Zu chimed in.

We had all disappointed Chevy somehow and knowing he was leaving Zoo only made shit worse.

"My apologies Chev. We fucked up," I said to him.

He looked at me. "I know you did it Foe. I told you we only kill unless we have to. You didn't listen." He shook his head, then pinched the bridge of his nose. "I'm leaving Cali," he blurted out.

Zu sat up, "The fuck you mean you leaving Cali? Nigga where you going?"

Diamond shook his head. "I thought it was Zoo over everything!"

"It's something I have to do for me. If Gods will I'll be back."

I heard Preach suck his teeth. "Then we all going!"

Chevy waved his hand. "Nah this trip is for me. Y'all got each other. I'm taking the Chevy I'll be good. Let's get through this race so we can move on."

If Chevy really thought we were letting him ride alone, he should have known better. I wanted to talk to though Harvey because she had to know and didn't say a single fucking word.

Chapter Eleven

HARVEY
Last Ride

I had just finished up my last client rushing to get to the race. It was Chevy's last time racing, and I refuse to miss it. Him bailing them all out of jail was his last straw. It gave him more reason to go on this trip. I wanted to talk to him after the race so he could at least talk to guys clearing things up. Chevy not opening up to them made things kind of hard. He and Zu still weren't on the best of terms, and I hadn't seen him hanging around the other guys. Nobody knew what the hell he was going through because he refused to say anything. After this race, I was going to force him to talk to me.

I hurried, making my way through the building. The sound of Foe's voice startled me.

"Why you ain't say shit!"

I placed my hand over my chest, trying to calm down. I giggled. "You scared me."

He stepped up to me, and his face showed he was pissed. "You knew that he was planning to leave Cali and you didn't say shit!"

"Remember it isn't my business to tell. He told y'all when he was ready," I said, now walking off.

I stormed out of the building to my car. Foe grabbed my arm, swinging me his way so fast I tripped and fell into him. When I lifted our lips were so close if I would have poked them out, kissing would have been the first thing we did. The way he looked at me was the same way he looked at me at the lounge. *What was this?* My heart began racing, my stomach fluttered. This feeling didn't happen with Zu. I straightened myself up, clearing my throat. "Don't you have a race to get to while you're in my face."

Foe hadn't blinked. "I'm where I need to be right now. Tell me where he going?"

I said nothing. "Harvey!" He yelled.

"Toussaint! He going to Toussaint!"

Confusion sat on his face. I knew he was trying to figure out why, but that was as much as I was willing to tell him. I unlocked my car door to get it, but wanted to say bye. "I will see you at the race?"

"Do you have feeling for him?" He suddenly asked.

I turned to him, "What?"

"I said do you have feelings for Zu?"

I swallowed deep. I like Zu a lot. He fucked up a few times, but he wasn't a bad person. I opened my mouth to say something, but Foe didn't allow me to. "I'll see you at the race."

He walked off to his bike. A part of me wanted to stop him, to tell him to come back so we could talk about whatever this was we were feeling. I know he felt the same thing I did when we looked at each other. *Did Foe and I like each other?* I ignored the feeling as I drove off, headed to their race.

By the time I pulled up, there were people everywhere. I got out of the car, scurrying over to the crowd. I squeezed my way through people to get to the front. Zoo's crowd was cheering, and they hadn't even showed up yet. I watched the other bikers, who look like they were ready for business. One of them was zooming up and down the street doing tricks, building excitement. They had women on their team with Dragon heat jackets on.

The sound of bikes approaching fueled the crowd behind me. I was on board this time. *"We don't fuck with you; we only fuck with da Zoo!"*

They pulled up, showing off as they usually did. Zu pulled his helmet off and I was expecting him to look at me, but he didn't. He held the most serious expression on his face. Something about him not acknowledging me made me feel some type of way. The girls began tussling me, shoving me to the side. Foe had to be watching me because I went to say something as he pulled me from the crowd. "You good?"

I nodded my head. "Aight then, smile. Zu sees you he has a lot riding on this race."

Foe went to go back to the crew and his hand slid down to mine, slowly gliding across my fingertips as he walked off. The shit made my body shuttered. I didn't know what was going on, but it scared me. *Zu was my person, wasn't he?*

I saw Zu and Chevy walking over to Dragon heat. They said a few words, then parted ways. Zu and Chevy grilled each other the entire time back to their bikes. All of this was giving me a bad feeling, but I shook it off. Zu had finally seen me and jog over. "Hey baby," I cooed.

"Sup, you Ok.?" He asked.

"Yes, give me a kiss," I told him.

I needed him to take my mind off the energy Foe and I passed through each other. I wanted him to show me that my mind was playing tricks on me. Zu leaned forward, pecking me on the lips. Normally, he was aggressive when kissing me, but not this time. I lowered my eyes then raise them only to catch Foe watching then pulled his eyes away. I glanced at Zu, then back at Foe. *You're going to be okay.* He mouthed.

The way I was feeling, I should have just left because this entire situation was making me sick by the second.

ZU

Tonight, the pressure was on. This single race would determine my friendship and I needed to remain focus. Chevy and I, not being on good terms, fucked with me. He was my brother, the nigga I could shoot the shit with, smoke with, talk to if I needed advice, and although he didn't turn his back on me fully, he had somewhat shut me out.

The juice bar was on the line and over hundred grand. After talking to Tony, Chevy said nothing. He sat on his bike, waiting to ride. Seeing Harvey was nice, and I know she wanted more attention, but now wasn't the time. Once the race was over, then I could give her all the attention she wanted, even some dick, if I was feeling up to it. Diamond and Preach were talking about God. Foe, he was sitting there off in his own world.

I could see none of us were focus. Tony had now called out so the race could begin. Chevy moved his bike to the center along with one of the Dragon Heat riders. I wanted to give him some sort of pep talk, but I knew he didn't want to hear it. I paced back and forth as they were getting ready to take off.

"Chill my nigga, Chevy's gone do what he's going to do," Foe said to me.

I had to do something. I slid my helmet on. "Yo Chev. Nigga you good?"

It was silent. He said nothing. *Fuck!* "Chevy!" I called out again.

He revved up his bike, building smoke. "Nigga let's ride!" he shouted as he took off.

My heart was racing as he sped off into the night. I could see Diamond taking off. We wanted to watch him make sure he was good. "Diamond talk to me?"

"This nigga fast I'm trying to keep up!" he shouted.

Harvey came over to me. "Babe, what's going on?" I heard her but ignored her.

She pulled on my jacket. "Oh, shit I—"

"Zu!" Harvey shouted.

I quickly took my helmet off. "What Harvey damn! You keep calling my name I'm trying to focus!" I yelled at her.

I wasn't trying to be on that type of time, but I was stressed. My friendship depended upon this race. Harvey said nothing as she walked away from me.

"Fuck! Harvey!" I called out.

She didn't bother to turn around. She continued to walk until she disappeared in the crowd. I wanted to chase after her, but I couldn't. I put my helmet back on. "Diamond, talk to me nigga."

"They're headed back and it ain't looking too good, this nigga dusting his ass."

I took my helmet off. *"Fuck!"* I screamed.

I could see Tony smiling from where he stood. Both set of bike lights began approaching us. *Come on Chev, come on!*

As they became closer, I was on the edge running up. The other rider was in front of Chevy. I just dropped my head because the shit was over. Not only was I about to lose my best friend, but his business. I heard Foe screaming, "Yeah nigga!"

I glanced up to Chevy doing a wheely. His bike slammed down as he sped up, winning the race by a fucking hair. He drifted his bike, creating tire marks on the pavement. *"We don't fuck with you; we only fuck with da Zoo!"* *"We don't fuck with you; we only fuck with da Zoo!"* everyone cheered.

Tony stepped over to Chevy as he removed his helmet. They shook hands and parted ways. With everything we've been through in the last couple of weeks, you would have thought Chevy would smile. Even with him winning this race, the nigga didn't crack one smile. I had to humble myself as I stepped up to him. "Chev my nigga I apologize," I said tapping my chest.

"Zu you put my business in jeopardy something I worked hard for. You almost cost us over a hundred bands had I lost this race. I respect you trying to apologize, but right now I'm not fucking with you. I'm. out. Of. Zoo," he finished walking off.

I stood there, ready to air the entire spot out. My friend and my girl walked away from me. Here I was trying to do the right thing to only be slapped in the face at the end.

I had to apologize to Harvey so she wouldn't leave Zu-Topia. Also, figure out a way to get back in Chevy's good graces and pray he would come back to Zoo....

Letters To My Reader

We have reached the end of the introduction. We have a lot to dive into going forward. So, get yourself ready for a Zoo fall/winter! As this story unfolds, I will drop books until I feel their story is complete. I wanted to give an insight on how they are together. Although they will still be together because they are a brotherhood. I think it's time to dive into each one of them to see what they really hitting for.

Again, I appreciate all the love I received on my boys. Thank you for trusting my pen! This was completely unexpected journey but I never back down on a challenge. I won't tell you here what's next, just expect the unexpected. You can always follow me on my socials or visit my site: www.authortatiana.com for updates.

Tiktok: Fresheebabii
IG: Freshiebabii/authortatiana

Til the next one, fairies!!

Made in United States
Troutdale, OR
11/25/2024

25287886R00124